Living
the
Dream

Marcie Shumway

Chapter One

Present Day

"Dreams are yours and no one else's,
they are your deepest passions coming to light."

The slit in my dress rode up my tan leg as I crossed my left over my right to get more comfortable. The large hand sitting on my thigh shifted as well, a finger running up the seam and over my bare skin. Chills ran through me, straight to my core. I pursed my lips together and settled my hand over his to halt his movements. Out of the corner of my eye I caught his smirk and I couldn't help but smile a bit as well. I was happy that he could still be his playful self, despite the nerves coursing through both of us.

I didn't know if I would ever get used to all the hoopla surrounding an awards show: the hair, the make-up, the dress clothes, the heels, the red carpet, the noise, the lights, the pictures, and the high energy. There was just so much going on and so much to take in. I almost missed being able to watch them from the comfort of my own couch in my pajamas. Almost.

The silky cobalt blue material I wore set off my eyes that were outlined in blue and black. It showed off my curves since it was form fitting and it had a low-cut bodice that teased the eyes, yet didn't reveal too much. Four inch stilettos in the same color as my dress accented my toned caves and gave my legs the appearance of being much longer than they actually were. Tendrils of blonde hair escaped my up-do and tickled my face as my date shifted beside me.

He was the reason we were here. This 6'4" bearded nervous wreck. His fingers began to drum against my leg. I rested my hand on top of his once again to calm him and smiled fully when our wedding rings *tinged* off each other. It wasn't the first time he had been nominated for an award, but it was the first time he had been up for Entertainer of the Year.

As the singer on one stage finished his set, an actor and a female country singer came out on another. All eyes were on them as they started talking because they were presenting the largest award of the night. My husband turned his hand over and intertwined our fingers, squeezing tightly. The two started to list off the nominees. It was not an easy field to be up against. The five contenders were amazing artists and some were good friends. It was a battle to be supportive of everyone. His left leg started jiggling against mine so I quickly put my free hand on it.

"And the ACM Entertainer of the Year is..."

His grip became so constricting that my fingers started to pulse.

"Knox Pride!"

I almost thought I had heard wrong until he hauled me to my feet. I grabbed his face in my hands and kissed him, hard. Tears streamed down my own. The emotions running through me were nearly more than I could bear. I was so proud of this man. He had worked so long and hard for this.

Knox made his way to the stage to accept his award and

was bombarded along the way with hugs and handshakes from fellow artists, song writers, and producers. His cheeks were pink with excitement and his smile ran ear-to-ear across his handsome face. When they handed it to him, I saw the tears well up in his brown eyes even from where I was sitting, causing mine to fill as well.

"First of all, I need to thank my biggest fan, my wife. This year has been everything it has because of her. I love you, Mackenzie!"

I blew him a kiss and wondered if he realized that he would have won this award with or without me in his life. The man was just plain talented, on top of being gorgeous, and the right people had finally noticed. As I listened to him give his short speech, someone filled his seat and grabbed my hand from my lap. I looked up and found Rebecca, one of the other nominees, sitting there with a huge grin herself and dried tears on her cheeks. My guess was that they were from her loss along with her happiness for him.

I couldn't help but be totally bewildered as I sat there with her while Knox headed to the back of the stage. The next act came out and Rebecca stood up to dance along with much of the crowd. My life had taken a total turn in the past year and a half, and as I stood beside this beautiful new friend of mine, I felt so grateful. I had a wonderful husband, amazing friends, and a growing career. Who would have known that a night in a small Nashville bar could turn in to this?

Chapter Two

A year and a half earlier...

"When life hands you an unexpected gift,
take it and run."

"You know there are some good-looking guys at this bar, Mackenzie," my friend, Kelly, piped up as we line danced to a 90's country song.

"I know," I told her, almost missing my step and bumping hips with one of our friends in the process.

"Not everyone has to be happy and in love like you, Kel," Meghan teased from my other side.

"Feeling that way isn't a bad thing, ya know," Alicia muttered from beside Kelly.

"Ladies, no fighting," I chided with a laugh. "I'll get back there. Right now, let me wallow and be carefree."

The four of us had been friends since grade school and despite the distance of college and our varying adult lives, we had remained close. This trip was so all of us could get away from everything going on back home for a bit. Kelly was soon-to-be Mrs. Shaw, Meghan had just lost her job though I had plans for her, Alicia was newly engaged, and I had recently gotten out of a five-year relationship. Though we probably could have gone closer to Maine than Tennessee.

As I looked around at them I couldn't have been more thankful. There was no way I could have made it through my current situation without them. I also had to chuckle at the differences between us all. Meghan was as tomboy as they came with her brown hair in a pixie cut and hazel eyes, while I was the leggy blonde-haired blue eyed beauty. Kelly was the spitfire redhead with green eyes and Alicia completed our foursome with her brown eyes, dark skin and hair.

We watched as a group of guys came in and sat at the bar facing the dance floor. All of them wore comfortably worn jeans and boots with t-shirts. Nothing that really stood out. I hated feeling like I was being watched, but I could have sworn that one of them looked vaguely familiar. He had his black baseball cap tugged low on his head and his solid build had to be over six feet.

"See," Kelly said elbowing me.

I rolled my eyes and altered my pace as the beat changed. The four of us remained for a few more songs and then went back to the table where our jackets were. Our supper had arrived along with a round of drinks and we dug in. The food was great, pub style, and the atmosphere was friendly and welcoming. The place wasn't very big size wise, yet the country décor gave it an open, larger feel.

As the night progressed we floated back and forth between the dance floor and our table. A small section of the floor remained for line dancing while the rest had opened up for couples and large groups. Meghan and I had danced with a few cowboys, however they started to get overly affectionate the more the alcohol flowed and we backed off. I caught the group at the bar moving down to the side of the dance floor out of the corner of my eye. The seemingly familiar man was definitely at least 6'4" and the black shirt and blue jeans he wore showed off his compact build even more.

"Come dance with me, sweetheart," a slurred voice requested grabbing my arm and pulling me in to turn me away from the men I had been watching

"I'm all set. Thank you though," I responded kindly while spinning away.

Unfortunately, he didn't take my hint. I felt his hand grip my arm, tighter this time, and I was pinned against his chest. His other arm wrapped around my waist like a vice grip. The stench of whiskey coming from this mouth due to his heavy breathing was nauseating. I tried mercilessly to free myself, but even in his drunken state he wasn't having it.

"Please let me go," I begged, borderline panicking.

I could see the girls in my peripheral vision. They were being detained by the cowboy's friends from the looks of it. Now, every bad dream I had had about this trip was coming back at me full force, along with everything my mother had warned me about. Visions of being abducted to being molested, flashed through my head. I tried one last time to pull away from him, only to have his arms tighten painfully around me.

"How about you let me cut in?" came a voice from behind me.

It was the guy that I had thought looked familiar. I felt the man I was being held by start to answer but he suddenly released me and hurried off. I stood there dumbfounded for a second before I was pulled into another set of arms. A warm, muscular, inviting set. I looked up into the eyes of my rescuer and was shocked at what I saw.

My breath caught and I had to remind myself to exhale. This wasn't just any man. It was a famous one as well as an attractive one. It was Knox Pride, only one of my favorite country singers that we had tickets to see in a small private concert the following night.

"Thank you for saving me," I said as the song changed and a much slower tune filled the air.

"You looked like you needed it," he replied matter-of-factly, putting his hands on my hips and pulling me closer.

"Does Knox Pride play white knight frequently?" I teased melting against his chest and wrapping my arms around his neck.

I felt him stiffen for a second when I said his name, yet the light tone I used seemed to instantly relax him. Clearly, he was out for a night with friends and wanted to do so without his celebrity status getting in the way. With our height differences he had to lean down a bit to hear me and to whisper into my ear.

"How bout we keep that our little secret?"

I nodded and enjoyed the music. Though it was hard to appreciate it when my insides were all in knots. I was currently being held snugly against the solid muscular body of a very famous man. Most women would kill to be in my position. I was just trying not to vomit all over him and ruin the intoxicating smell of a woodsy cologne and Old Spice deodorant.

When the song ended we untangled from each other. Before I could start to thank him, he placed his hand on the small of my back and ushered me back to my table where the girls were buzzing with anticipation of the details of my dance. As I pulled out my chair to sit down, I noticed that Knox's group had moved to a table near ours. He tipped the bill of his cap towards me and joined them.

"Ummm, so what just happened?" Alicia asked leaning towards me to keep our voices from carrying, not that they could actually hear us over the loud music if they wanted to.

"I was just saved from a drunken cowboy," I replied trying

to keep myself from gawking at the table behind me like a star struck fool.

"Yes, you were," Kelly shrieked and pointed out, "but that wasn't just any man saving you!"

"No, it wasn't. Let's not make a big deal of it," I hissed as her voice had been loud enough to be heard by those close to us.

I saw the confusion on all of their faces. They wanted to gush about what had happened, yet I couldn't do it. Not when I had felt his stress at being recognized. The gossip could wait until we got back to the hotel room. Instead I turned the conversation to the guy that I had seen Meghan dancing with. They had had just enough alcohol that it wasn't hard to deter them.

Not long after I had sat down, one of our favorite songs from 2006 came on and we were back on the dance floor. Laughing as Kelly hip checked me during our line dance, I looked up and found Knox watching me from his table. Our eyes locked and I felt my cheeks warm. I focused my attention back on the girls. I didn't want to seem like a psycho stalker, though I could look into those soulful eyes all night long if I had the opportunity.

A few songs later we started to head back to grab our stuff and settle up our tab. We were tired and ready to go rest up for the concert the following night. One of Knox's slower ballads came on and the next thing I knew, I was being guided back to the dance floor by a hand lightly around my wrist. When I could focus my eyes, I found that Knox himself was the one pulling me along.

When we reached an open spot, he pulled me to his chest and wrapped his arms around my waist. As he settled his hands on the small of my back I put my arms around his neck once again. I didn't want to break the spell so I placed my cheek against his shirt and moved with him. My friends stood by our table staring at us in wonderment. Rather than let their wide eyes ruin anything, I closed mine.

I started to hear a rumble beneath my ear. Knox had started singing quietly along with the song about heartache from one special night. I had my own personal concert. His baritone voice sent heat pooling to my woman parts. It was hard to remind myself this was a one-time thing. I shifted to bring my ear closer to his mouth and cupped one hand around the back of his neck while the other toyed with his hair. His hands started to travel up and down my back sending shivers down my spine.

The song ended and neither of us rushed to get out of the embrace. He squeezed me tightly against his body in a quick hug before releasing me. When my hands came down from his shoulders one of his hands reached for mine and intertwined our fingers together. A shock ran up my arm and my eyes snapped up to his. He smiled softly and tugged me towards the tables where our friends were waiting.

"So, I am doing this concert tomorrow night," Knox told me as I let go of his hand and reached for my lightweight jacket on the back of a chair.

I raised my eyebrow at him in curiosity while I shrugged into it. I could hear Meghan chatting with some of his friends behind me while the other girls went to pay up the bill. Knox tucked his hands into his pockets and shuffled his feet in what I could only take as a nervous gesture. It was sweet.

"I would love to give you ladies some tickets if you would give me your number."

"Well, we already have plans," I informed him with a sly smile.

"Oh," he stuttered as his face fell.

"We already have tickets to your concert," I told him laughing.

"That's great!"

His face had lit up with the confession. I didn't want to get excited because I was pretty sure the alcohol consumed tonight was a major factor in the chemistry between us. However, I was fine with playing this game out until we left.

"How about giving me your number?"

"I'll tell you what. If you give me your phone, I will put my number in it. If you remember who I am tomorrow, you can text me or call me."

Knox wasted no time in pulling his phone from his back pocket and unlocking the screen before handing it to me. A picture of his sister and his nephew graced the wallpaper and I smiled before clicking on the contacts button. I finished putting my information in and handed it back to him. He took it, letting our fingers slide against each other before he pulled away and pocketed the phone. I smiled shyly and turned to head towards my friend.

"I won't forget you that easily," he whispered in my ear as he came up beside me to join his friends as well.

I blushed before I could stop it and his low chuckle rumbled beside me. Meghan's hand was out for mine when I got to her and I took it appreciatively. Allowing her to pull me along, I looked over my shoulder one last time and found Knox's eyes on me. I smirked at him and turned back to find the other two girls waiting for us by the door. As soon as we were reunited, I fell into the role of giddy girl and started to spill about my one night with a super star.

* * *

Marcie Shumway

Living the Dream is available on Amazon - in ebook and paperback!

Chapter Three

"A friendship bonds you for a time,
a sisterhood bonds you for life."

"Her phone keeps buzzing," I heard Kelly whisper. "Someone needs to wake her up."

I tried to keep my eyes closed and refrain from laughing, but their chatter was making it hard. I knew my phone was vibrating, signaling a text message. I wasn't too worried about it; however, I had listened to my nosey girlfriends theorize about who the message was from for the past half hour. I was pretty sure it was my mother, yet listening to them had been highly entertaining.

"Oh my gosh!" I finally exclaimed, opening my eyes and reaching for my phone causing all three of them to jump.

"You're up?" Alicia stammered putting her hand over her heart.

"How could I sleep with you Betty's clucking so loud?" I asked giving them a mock glare as I unlocked my screen.

"We're living vicariously through you with this country

star, so hurry up all ready," Meghan stated climbing onto my bed and practically sitting on me.

"It's probably just my mom...," I started and trailed off when I realized that was not the case.

I had received one message at two o'clock in the morning, about an hour after we had returned from the bar. It was from a number that I didn't have saved in my phone and the area code was from a different state than mine. Based on the message, I could only assume it was Knox. It read...

I told you, you're not that easy to forget.

I slapped my hand over my mouth and kicked my feet nearly unseating Meghan. They all knew what my reaction meant and went diving for my phone. Kelly ended up with it and, as I laughed hysterically, she read it to the others.

How did I react to that? What did that mean? I wasn't exactly sure what to think, but I was enjoying this electrifying feeling. It was much better than the down and depressed ones that I had been having lately. Even if nothing became of this, which I was sure it wouldn't, I really wanted to float for a while. My brain started humming with all the possible outcomes and I realized the girls were chatting around me.

"What?" I asked shaking my head to clear it.

"I think he is just trying to get into your pants," Alicia commented. "Something seems weird about this."

"How come you are all of the sudden changing your tune?" I snapped, grabbing my phone back from Kelly. "I'm sure if he was just after a piece of ass that he could have any one of thousands of groupies at his shows."

"We just watched you go through hell when you and Brandon split. I am not going to apologize for watching out for you."

"Maybe this is exactly what I need! Something to get my mind off all of that. It was been six months and I am ready to shake it off," I told them all as I got up and headed to the bathroom. "Please just let me enjoy this."

Shutting the door smartly behind me, I leaned against it and pinched the bridge of my nose between my thumb and forefinger. Alicia had always been the mother hen and I knew where she was coming from, but I was my own person. A little flirting and casual touching with a man wasn't going to break me all over again. We were leaving in a few days and I wanted to enjoy the rest of the trip with my friends. Taking a deep breath, I opened the door and stepped back out into the room.

"Listen..."

"We're sorry..."

"I crossed a line..."

"We love you..."

We laughed as we all started talking at once. This was the reason we had remained so close. Fights didn't last long and we all were quick to apologize. None of us liked confrontation or having other people upset with us. It was the one thing that we did have in common. Gathering in a group hug, the minor spat was quickly forgotten.

"So, what are you going to say?" Kelly finally asked with her eyebrow raised.

"How do you even respond to that?" Meghan threw in sitting back down on my bed.

"With something smart and witty," Alicia chimed in.

I giggled and sat down next to Meghan, knee to knee. Swiping my fingers across the screen, I opened the text message again and prepared to type. I wanted to be amusing, but that wasn't me. It had been years since I had had to flirt with anyone. I did want to say something that wouldn't make me look like a total fool since we would be seeing him again tonight at the concert. Finally, I came up with something.

How about when you are sober? ☺

"Real original," Meghan snorted falling back on the bed.

"Hey! I am out of practice," I reminded her throwing a pillow.

Putting my phone on the night stand, I tried not to focus on it while we made our plans for the day. It was already pushing ten o'clock and we had the concert at seven. It was decided we would grab brunch through room service and then do a spa day before heading over to the venue early. It was being held at a pub, so we figured we would just grab supper there before the show.

Our food arrived while we were all cleaning up and putting on comfortable clothes. Meghan and Alicia had opted for just manicures and pedicures, while Kelly and I came to the conclusion that we wanted both along with massages. I was so looking forward to having the kinks worked out of my muscles from the stress back home and the traveling. It had been too long since I had taken some time for myself and unwound.

"Phones," Alicia stated putting her hands out.

"What?!" Kelly sputtered as I turned mine over without question.

"No phones today," Alicia told her. "Today is about vegging out. Nothing from back home to distract us."

Meghan handed hers to our friend with a shrug and went back to eating. I laughed when Kelly tried to argue with her. Kel was in the "puppy love" stage of her relationship due to her upcoming nuptials and she never went long without talking to Matt. I, on the other hand, was more than happy to oblige. If it kept me from obsessing about whether or not Knox texted me back, I was game.

Kelly and Matt had been together for six years. Matt, being my older brother, had always had to deal with us girls following him and his best friend, Brandon, around everywhere. Somewhere along the lines Kelly had fallen for his blonde hair and green eyes. He had fought it for almost a year before she had caught him under the mistletoe at a family party. The rest was history.

When Kelly finally stopped being stubborn and gave her phone to Alicia, we packed our bags and headed out with flip flops on our feet for the pedicures. The beautiful 70-degree weather was fantastic; we couldn't have picked a better place to vacation knowing that it was about 40 degrees back home. The spa was only a block away, so we decided to walk to it. While the girls gabbed I got lost in our surroundings.

I definitely wasn't a city girl, but something about this one I loved. I'm not sure if it was because I knew it was the birthplace of country music or if it was because of the energy that oozed from it. The smells of the water, cigar smoke, and fried food filled my nostrils. I took a deep breath and smiled to myself. I couldn't wait to see it at night with all the signs lit up.

"What are you grinning about?" Meghan asked.

Looking at her, I realized we had stopped in front of Cassie's Place which is where our appointments were for. I shook my head and we followed Alicia and Kelly into the building. Soft meditation music filled the air and multiple spices could be smelt. We didn't even get a chance to sit. We were immediately ushered away to various rooms down a long hallway. Let the day of relaxation begin.

A couple of hours later Kelly and I sat in our pedicure chairs reading *People* magazines, totally lax. The massages had been amazing and all my muscles were soft and supple. Meghan and Alicia were across the room having their manicures done and gabbing with the ladies. My ears suddenly perked up when I heard Knox's name in the conversation.

"Yeah, we are going to the concert too," the curvy blonde working on Meghan's nails told her as she popped her gum.

"We are going to go really early so that we can sit up front and I can give him my number."

Out of the corner of my eye, I saw Kelly look at me with her brows raised. I picked my magazine up a little higher so that they couldn't see my smile and I shushed her so I could continue to listen. I had to know where this was going.

"Oh really?" Meghan asked with a chuckle.

"Yep," she replied running a file along my friend's hand. "That is the whole reason I moved here, so that I could gobble me up one of those rich hottie singers."

I slapped the magazine against my face and laughed silently. The woman working on my feet did as well. When I pulled the book away, Kelly was covering her face and the brunette at her feet was rolling her eyes. Oh, the dreams of the young. She didn't want Knox because he was him, she wanted a sugar daddy and by the sounds any good-looking man would do.

We finished up at Cassie's, generously tipping the ladies that had done our manicures and pedicures. We giggled heading back out onto the street as we talked about the young blonde and her dreams. I hoped the reality of life didn't come back and bite her on the ass. Heck, mine had.

"So, what are you wearing tonight?" Alicia asked everyone as we reached the hotel and headed inside.

"I'm thinking about that purple sequined top we picked up yesterday along with my jeans and boots," Kelly told her pushing the third-floor button when we stepped inside the elevator.

The conversation continued about attire and hair until we made our way back to our suite. Grabbing my phone from the bowl on the table by the door where we had left them, I headed to get my clothes from my suitcase. I had decided on dark boot cut jeans, a flowy sleeveless navy blue top that made my eyes stand out, and my black cowboy boots. Even if I didn't catch Knox's attention, I was going to look good. Locking myself in the bathroom I showered and started prepping for the night.

Not until I was dressed and straightening my hair with the flat iron did I think to check the messages on my phone. I had one from each of my parents, checking in, which had me smiling. Despite being 26 years old, they still worried about me. Scrolling down, I found that I had one from Knox. Opening it with shaking hands, I beamed.

Even when I'm sober ☺ *Meet me for appetizers after the show?*

"Girls!!!!"

Chapter Four

"The way a man kisses you can tell you everything,
his raw desires and thoughts are all out there for you to see."

At five o'clock that night we entered The Bull's Horns.
I had been right about the walk over. The whole
block was lit up with neon signs. The reflections
bounced off the water and the energy and smells were intensi-
fied from that morning. It was simply amazing. I was definitely
glad we had come early because the place was already filling
up. The show wasn't for another couple of hours, but it was first
come, first serve seating.

We found a tall bar table at the back of the room and made
ourselves comfortable. It was a small enough space that there
wasn't a bad seat anywhere. There was another row of tables
behind us and around 50 chairs in front of us. All the regular
tables had been removed. Chairs were already covered in
purses and jackets to reserve them while people milled about
with drinks. Others had the same idea we did and were

ordering food. I think most people were hoping for a glimpse of Knox or his band ahead of time.

Our waitress was just leaving, having taken our drink and food order, when I caught sight of the woman from the spa. Sure enough she and her friend had arrived early enough to score two seats directly in front of the stage. I pointed her out to the others and we all laughed. If only she knew who I had danced with the night before.

"Oh ladies!" she gushed coming over.

As she got closer I noticed her attire, glammed up cowgirl with pants so tight I didn't even know how she got in them, a button up shirt that was straining against her chest, and brand new boots that were straight out of the box and covered in rhinestones. This was what they considered a groupie through and through. I was hard pressed to see what a man like Knox would want with a woman like that, one trying to be something she wasn't. Meghan clearly had the same thought since she snorted beside me. I bumped her leg with mine under the table and bit my lip to keep from laughing as they reached our group.

"This will never do! You ladies will never get to meet the guys way back here!"

"We're fine," Kelly told them with a chuckle, along with filling them in on her and Alicia's relationship status'.

After finding out Meghan and I were single, her eyes immediately turned on me. I made a mental note to get Kelly back for that later. Before I could say anything, my phone signaled a text message. She turned to Meghan as I used the excuse "it might be important" to check it. I had to slap my hand over my mouth to contain a giggle when I read the message. It was a response from Knox after I had returned a text accepting his invitation for food later and letting him know that Meghan would be there to supervise.

Thanks for the vote of confidence LOL I'll find someone to keep her occupied ;) See you after the show!

"Who was that from?" Meghan asked as soon as our visitors left the table.

"That was our date for after the show," I informed her with a grin.

I caught the look in Alicia's eye and I leaned over to cover her hand with mine to give it a squeeze. I knew that she was concerned, which was the reason that I had asked Meghan to hang back with me after so I could meet up with the singer. I wasn't stupid enough to do it alone, yet I was curious enough to want to know what would happen if I did see him. She flashed me a smile in return.

Our food was quick to arrive despite the number of people around us. I had ordered a bacon burger with onion rings; if I was going to go to a pub I was going to get pub food. It was the best burger I had had in a long time. It was perfectly cooked and the onion rings were smothered in thick batter. We ate in silence as we took in everything going on. The crowd had increased as had the noise.

Just as we were finishing up, the band started to come out to get their instruments ready. I recognized a couple from the night before. People started to make their way back to their seats as soon as they saw them, quickly relieving the congestion around our table. The waitress came over, cleared our dishes away, and took another round of drink orders.

Suddenly, the energy in the room seemed to shift and before I even saw him, I knew Knox had stepped up to the stage. Tonight he had on black boots, dark wash boot cut jeans, and a black t-shirt. The colors showed off his solid build and every woman in the room was drooling. His smile was ear-to-ear. The man clearly loved what he did.

"Good evening everyone! Are we ready to listen to a little acoustic music and have a good time?" he asked settling in on a stool with his guitar.

His deep voice sent a chill down my spine and my lady parts instantly sprang to life. Maybe meeting him after wasn't the best idea. I was likely to turn into a lunatic groupie by the time the show was over and make a complete fool of myself in front of him. A sigh escaped me as he strummed a few cords and talked to his band behind the mic.

When the start of my favorite song by him "She's All Mine" began to play, my heart started to pound. The soft crooning of his voice had every female member of the audience, and probably some men, pooling into puddles of goo. I had listened to his albums over and over again, but none of them did justice to his singing live and acoustic at that. I had gotten a taste of it the night before when we had been dancing, however, it was totally different when he was on stage. He owned the room.

I couldn't take my eyes off from him. The song started to wind into the last two verses and that's when his eyes found mine across the room. I would have mistaken it for him just looking around at everyone, yet the corner of his mouth turned up into a smirk and he nodded subtly. I felt my cheeks get flush and Kelly smacked my arm lightly from beside me so I knew that they had seen it too.

He picked up the tempo for the next few songs, bringing those around us in the back to their feet and those in their chairs to stomping and clapping. When he brought it back down a bit for the sixth song of the set he talked about his family. He was usually very private about them; however, he had recently become an uncle and by the look on his face, was very excited about it. His sister, Bella, and her husband had welcomed a baby boy into the family. Performing this show so close to home had allowed him to meet his new nephew and spend time with the new family. This led him into a song about the power and love of family called "Just Ask" and I swear there wasn't a dry eye in the house, us included.

I finally turned back to the girls when Knox and the band took a ten-minute break in the middle of the show, they were slated to play for another forty-five minutes. I had barely made myself comfortable when Alicia pointed towards Knox and gestured for me to look. Evidently our "friends" had taken the intermission as the perfect time to do a meet-and-greet despite being told that the band would be available after the show. Looking over my shoulder to pretend I wasn't necessarily looking at them, I could see the blonde draping herself on Knox and I just about fell out of my chair when I saw her slip her hand and a piece of paper into his front pocket. His face was priceless and he was quick to plaster a smile back on.

"Did you see that?" Kelly hissed.

"That is one brave woman," I stated nodding and turning myself around. I didn't need to see any more.

The band settled back in and when I heard them start to tune their guitars I turned back. The women in the front were gigging behind their hands and eyeing Knox like a piece of meat. I rolled my eyes and when I focused on the stage again I found myself being watched. The knowing smile was quick before he shifted his attention to the rest of the audience. I felt my cheeks get warm from the embarrassment of being caught. The others laughed from behind me and I gave them a mock glare. Unfortunately, I couldn't keep a straight face when Meghan let out a snort.

Knox and the band immediately jumped into one of his newer songs "Carnival" that was fairly upbeat. It was a good thing considering the four of us were struggling to contain ourselves. It didn't take long for Kelly and I to jump up and dance with those around us. The music had a strong bass that was easy to move to and it just begged you to sing along.

The second half of the show seemed to go much quicker. Kelly and I had been up and down with the music so when the band finished the last song we were almost relieved. Meghan and I got a couple waters as the other two got their stuff together to leave. Everyone had remained on stage and they were readily signing autographs. I also noticed groupies, other than our overly enthusiastic friends, that were waiting around to try to get a chance to spend extra time with Knox or one of the guys. Sorry ladies tonight he was mine, well for a little while anyway.

Kelly and Alicia headed back to the hotel, leaving us with strict instructions to keep in touch via cellphone. We laughed at their protectiveness and assured them that we would be just fine. After the girls were gone, I made a beeline for the bathroom, only to get caught up in a line of people leaving. By the time I returned, the crowd had thinned considerably.

"I think you're going to have to share him," Meghan commented with a smirk as I sat down sideways in my chair, leaning on the back with my side.

I looked over towards the stage and found Knox being bombarded by the two women from the spa. Most of the band was gone except for Cort, Knox's brother, and one other man. They obviously thought it was entertaining to watch because they stood back smiling at his discomfort. I wasn't sure if it was my place to say something, but I did know I didn't plan on waiting all night. My energy reserve was running on low as it was.

Finally, when I had just about had enough waiting, I felt a warm hand on my back. I turned and looked up to find Knox standing beside me. He flashed his killer smile, laced with apology. I couldn't help but return it. He let out a breath and leaned down.

"What can I get you?" he asked, never moving his hand from the small of my back.

"Onion rings and water with lemon," I replied trying to keep my wits about me now that he was this close.

He nodded and moved to the bar, which was just a few steps away. When I turned back to Meghan I found her seat empty. Looking up farther, I noticed she had moved to a table with Cort and the other guy from the band that had been waiting for Knox. I raised my eyebrow at her only to receive a wink and a smile in return. Chuckling, I turned my attention back to the man I had patiently waited all night to see.

Knox stood with one foot resting on the step under the bar and his arms crossed in front of him on the mahogany counter top. His clothes were slightly damp with sweat from the show, but his woodsy cologne still tickled my nose from when he had been by the table. The muscles in his back moved beneath his t-shirt as he shifted and laughed with the bartender. That's when I noticed the slight dimple in his right cheek. Oh boy, was I goner now.

"Okay, food should be ready in 15," he informed me when he returned to the table.

"Sounds good," I replied playing with my wrapper after I had put the straw in my fresh glass. "Where did your girl-friends go?"

"I sent them packing, well I tried anyway," he assured me chuckling and ducking his head a bit.

"Does that happen at every show?"

"Unfortunately at most of them."

"Hmmmm."

"I'm not a playboy, if that's what you think."

My eyes snapped up at that comment and the frustration in

his voice. His face was almost sad and he took a long drink of his beer. He may have been a famous singer; however, he was also a man. A very sensitive, caring man obviously.

"I never said you were," I said softly, "I just don't know how a girlfriend or wife would deal with her man having all that attention all the time."

"Haven't had to worry about that yet," came the reply as his hand came down to cover mine and to intertwine our fingers. "I don't usually give my numbers to strange beautiful women either."

"Strange?" I asked with a teasing note causing him to laugh and his face to light back up.

The conversation turned to the show and how happy he was that it had all worked for him to play here. He loved smaller venues where he could get one-on-one time with his audience, not to mention the fact that he was closer to home. Our food came soon after and I dove into the onion rings, despite already having some earlier in the night.

"I love a woman with an appetite," Knox laughed as I reached over and swiped one of his fries.

I stuck my tongue out at him and continued to eat. While we were silent, I noticed that the music had changed from the upbeat current country songs to mellow 90s country. It was perfect. The beat slowed even more when "Love of My Life" by Sammy Kershaw filled the room. Before I knew what was happening, I was being pulled from my chair.

Knox tugged me between the tables and into his embrace. I brought my arms up his chest and around his neck, cupping one hand around while the other toyed with the waves on the back of his head just as I had done the night before. He let out a masculine purr and wrapped his arms around me tighter. I closed my eyes a bit and moved with him in time to the music.

Pulling away slightly to look me in the face, his eyes dipped to my lips and back up again.

"Can I kiss you?" he whispered.

I didn't know whether to laugh from the Casper movie reference or to cry in happiness and disbelief. Using my hands, I brought his head down until our lips met in a brief yet sweet kiss. It was just a brush or two of our lips against each other, however, the tingles ran through me and down my spine just the same. I opened my eyes and found him looking down at me with a content smile that flashed the dimple I had noticed earlier.

"So, what happens after tonight?" I asked once we had settled back down at the table and Knox had received a refill on his beer.

"I would like to hope that we can keep in touch," he stated. "Text messages, phone calls, FaceTime. Whatever works."

"Is this one of those times where we say we are going to keep in touch and it lasts a few weeks, maybe a month, and then things trickle to nothing?"

This time when Knox stood I was a little more prepared. He pulled me into his arms again, only this time there wasn't a slow song playing. Not sure what his intent was I put my hands on his chest for balance and found myself swept up into a passionate kiss. Where the first kiss had been sweet and soft, this one was filled with lust and fireworks. I gasped at the warmth that quickly spread down between my legs and he used the opportunity to dart his tongue into my mouth. Circling his around mine and stroking it, I shifted my head to change the angle of the kiss and balled my fists into this shirt.

A low groan came from deep within Knox and he wrapped his arms around my waist to lift me up off my feet. As he set me back down he ended it, moving so that our foreheads remained touching. We were both panting from the exchange and I closed my eyes for a moment to gather my thoughts and catch my breath.

"I repeat," he started, once he could talk, "I don't give my number to women or my cell phone for that matter. From that first moment I saw you and your friends on the dance floor I had to get to know you. There is something about you that draws me to you. I want to see where this goes."

"Wow," I stuttered. "Okay. I'm......okay."

Chuckling, Knox hugged me tightly and took me back to the table. I could hear Meghan arguing good naturedly with the guys about something sports related and that helped to level me. My head was spinning. I had not only been kissed by a gorgeous man, but he was famous and he wanted to get to know me.

"Can you pinch me?" I asked him.

"Honey, if you're dreaming then I am too."

I smiled at him shyly and yawned before I could stop myself. Slapping my hand across my mouth I felt my cheeks warm. I knew I was tired from the running around the past few days and the traveling, guess I just hadn't realized how tired. Laughing, Knox got up and reached for my hand. Following suit, I slipped my hand into his, intertwining our fingers, and grabbed my purse with my free one. He gestured to the other guys and we headed towards the door.

"Ace, my road manager, is going to make sure you ladies make it back to the hotel," he informed me once we got outside.

"Sounds good," I replied knowing why he couldn't go with us.

"I'll talk to you tomorrow," he promised pulling me into his arms and dropping a kiss on my nose.

"We are flying back, so if I don't answer, don't panic," I told him taking in his smell and the feel of him and committing it to memory.

He kissed me on the lips one more time just as Meghan and the men came out. He gave me a final hug and released me to my friend. With a wave, he and Cort walked away in the opposite direction and eventually around the corner of another building. The man that Knox had called Ace continued his gentle banter with Meghan as we headed towards our hotel. Linking my arm with hers I sighed and wondered how much my life had just changed without my really knowing it.

Chapter Five

*"Getting to know someone is the best part of any relationship,
every discovery is like a new present at Christmas."*

BEEP! BEEP! BEEP!

I rolled over and groped blindly for my alarm clock. My fingers finally found the button and I was rewarded with silence. Flopping onto my back once again, I slowly opened my eyes. It took me a few moments to get my bearings and register that I was in my own bed. We had arrived home later than planned the previous day and after dropping my bags I hit the bed without a conscious thought. I didn't even remember setting the alarm. The whole vacation still seemed like a dream.

Grabbing my phone from the charger, I did an internal battle of whether or not I could go back to sleep. That's when I heard the bang from outside and knew I needed to get up. Unfortunately, horses couldn't feed themselves. Dragging myself up with a sigh, I reached for my jeans, long-sleeved t-shirt, and sweatshirt that sat on my bureau. After a quick clean up and change, I was on my way downstairs with my hair up in a messy bun and my socks and cell phone in hand.

Part way down, two fur balls darted in front of me, startling me. Gripping the handrail, I cursed under my breath. Roy and Lightening were clearly ready for breakfast too. When I got my balance back, I continued to the bottom of the stairs. That's when I noticed my phone was flashing a blue light signaling a text message. When I got to the kitchen I put it down and figured I would check it before I made my way to the barn. First things first, coffee and food for the twins circling my legs.

"Okay, boys, I get it," I mumbled to the orange tabbies as I pulled down the handle on my Keurig and made my way to the refrigerator for their can of food.

Setting it on the counter, I reached down to get their dishes by the sliding glass door. I caught my horses watching me and stopped a minute. I hadn't realized how much I had missed all five of my fur-babies while I was gone. The three horses waited patiently along the fence, nickering loud enough that I could hear them through the closed door, while the cats still circled and rubbed against my legs. Closing my eyes for a moment I took a deep breath and inhaled the familiar berry/spice mixture that came from my wax plug-in warmers throughout the house. It was so good to be home.

Once I had the little boys settled in with their breakfast, I prepped my cup of coffee and leaned against the counter. Remembering the unread message on my phone, I leaned over and picked it up with my free hand. Clicking on the side button to turn my screen on I was shocked to see that the message, or messages rather, were from Knox. I hadn't heard from him at all while we were traveling home, despite his promise, and I had kept telling myself to just appreciate that I had had at least one amazing night with him.

Swiping my finger across the screen I found that I had two messages from him. The first one was an apology...

Sorry haven't texted sooner. Crunching in time with the family before I go back on the road. FaceTime tomorrow night?

Then when I didn't respond I think he got a little worried...

Kenzie? I'm so sorry. I hope you understand. I want to talk to you. Now I sound like a creepy stalker. Laughing, I sipped my coffee and sent him a message letting him know that I was up for FaceTime and apologizing for not getting back to him sooner. Finishing my cup, I put my phone down and just enjoyed the quiet. As much as I loved my girlfriends, I was more a solitary person by nature. Today I had nothing on the agenda other than relaxing and catching up from being on vacation. Putting my phone in my pocket and my cup in the sink, I went to the mat by the doors and pulled on my boots.

I was just pulling one open to step out when I felt a vibration against my hip. Thinking that there was no way Knox would be up now if he had messaged me so late the night before, I figured I would check it once I had the horses settled with their breakfast. As the cool fall air finished the job the coffee had started, I made my way across the lawn to the barn.

Entering through a door into the tack room, I felt my phone vibrate again. Smiling to myself, I grabbed the boys' rubber buckets from the shelf they were resting on and lined them up on the floor. My amazing mother had premixed the grain the night before so all I had to do was put in the beet pulp that had been soaking all night. She had also left me a large *I love you and miss you!* message on my dry erase board that had the grain rations written on it.

I walked through the door that led to the inside of the barn and could hear the boys outside getting impatient. Making my way past the four stalls, I got to the large overhead door and leaned over to grip the bottom and open it. Once I had, three noses pushed their way through the slats in the gate looking for breakfast and attention. I laughed patting each one briefly before I made my way to unlatch it and slip through. They all gave me my space as I turned to shut it behind me and walked towards the side of the barn to put the buckets down one by one, making sure to leave enough space that they weren't crowded together.

It always amazed me how easily they figured out their pecking order and who went where. It was always the same, Max the chestnut Quarter Horse, Gem the dapple-grey Thoroughbred, and Case the black Quarter Horse Cross. For the most part, I think Max was in charge and the other two just went along with the flow. Moving back into the barn I grabbed the wheelbarrow my mother had left filled with hay for me and went back out to put it into three separate piles for them. The routine was calming and the familiar smells warmed me.

When I had the pasture picked clean and the horses were munching on their hay, I leaned up against the wood fence and checked my phone. Both messages were from Knox. Surprised I opened the conversation.

Awesome! Seven o'clock your time okay?

I can't wait to see your beautiful face again ☺

Beaming, I messaged him back confirming the time and letting him know that I couldn't wait to see his handsome face either. As much as the compliment tickled me, I was still not sure where all of this was going. Pushing away from the fence, I pocketed my cell phone and turned towards the real "men" in my life. The ones that didn't talk back and that loved me no matter what. Brushing them all with soft brushes to remove the dust on their coats, I decided I needed to message the girls before tonight. They could give me some advice on how to handle all this.

Despite not having any plans for the day and my excitement over my FaceTime date, my day flew by. The next thing I knew, I was crawling into bed with a bowl of ice cream, my computer, and my cell phone. The cats were curled up at the bottom as I tucked my feet under the blankets and attempted to make myself comfortable. After talking with the girls, I had settled on pajama pants, a cami, and a zip-up hooded sweat-shirt. I wanted to be at ease and to not have to get up to get ready for bed once we were done talking.

My pony tail was bopping on my head as I ate a few bites of ice cream and started booting up my laptop. Just as I entered my username and password my phone started going off signaling me for a FaceTime session. Pushing the button without thinking, Knox's handsome face filled the screen. His hair was a mess and he looked tired, but the smile he flashed me had my heart skipping a beat. I returned it easily and picked up the phone to settle back against my pillows.

"Well, hello gorgeous," he greeted sitting back against the booth seat behind him, clearly he was on his bus and at the kitchen table.

"Hey," I responded shyly, feeling my cheeks get red with the praise. "You must be back on the road?"

"Yeah, headed to Virginia," came the reply.

"You look exhausted. Handsome but exhausted," I amended quickly.

"Gee, thanks."

"Sorry," I apologized flinching.

"It's okay," he chuckled, "I spent a lot of time with my family since I was close to home and the holidays will be quick visits due to touring."

"Now that you are on the road you can rest," I joked, shifting.

"Exactly. Cute jammies," Knox told me letting his voice go low.

"Thanks," I squeaked as the baritone sound burned a path right to my core.

"So, you know what I do for a living, but I don't think you ever told me what you do."

"What? You didn't google me?" I asked half kidding and laughing.

"You know what, I hadn't even thought of that," he said honestly.

Before he said anything else, I saw him pull his tablet over and I could see him keying on it with one hand as he still held his phone with the other. I saw him wait for Google to do the search of my name and then his face showed a range of emotions. I stifled a giggle as his eyes grew large and I saw everything from confusion to surprise to amazement flitter across his features.

"No way," he whispered to himself as his grin got larger causing the dimple to show on his right cheek.

"MacKenzie Shaw......You're a romance novelist?? A very well-known and best-selling one at that!"

"Yep," I confirmed, laughing because of the look of disbelief on his face.

"So, do I need to worry about being in one of these books?"

"No, no worries. I don't put anyone I actually know in my books. However, I can't help it if some characters have characteristics of those that I know and love."

"Huh. Maybe the better question is, should I read one to see what you like..."

I had just put a spoonful of ice cream in my mouth and was attempting to swallow when he uttered the last comment. It went down the wrong tube and I coughed and sputtered for a moment. My face felt like it was on fire and Knox was laughing so hard tears were starting to stream down his face.

"You're hilarious," I stated dryly as I rolled my eyes.

"I thought that was a good one," he stated trying to control himself.

We chatted for almost an hour and only called an end to the conversation because Knox was fighting to keep his eyes open. We talked about everything and nothing at all. I never once worried about what my hair looked like or how I was dressed like a total bum, nor did the exchange ever feel forced or awkward. Hanging up we promised we would try to FaceTime at least once a week, if not more, depending on what our schedules allowed. It was an honest try at dating over the web. I was just starting to fall asleep when I heard my phone vibrate. Reaching up to grab it, I turned it so I could read the screen without unplugging the device. It was Knox:

Good night beautiful xoxo

Good night handsome xoxo

Texting along with FaceTime continued more frequently than I thought they would for the next few weeks. Soon it was November and I had a few trips to make due to my new book coming out. Checking my calendar one day I decided to look and see if any of my traveling coincided with Knox's tour dates. I was surprised to find that he was going to be just outside of Boston the following week and so was I. Pulling up MapQuest I did a little digging and found that we were only going to be an hour and a half apart.

"Hey, Meghan," I called to my friend who was across the room typing away on her computer.

When we had returned home from our vacation I had hired her as my personal assistant. My writing had exploded and I couldn't keep up with ordering books and swag, scheduling, promos, and everything else that came with the job. It had been functioning better than I could have imagined. Normally working with friends would come back to haunt you, but the two of us had quickly fallen into a daily routine and it was great.

"What's up?" she asked turning fully to look at me.

"Do you have Ace's number by any chance?" I asked her referring to Knox's tour manager that she had seemed to click with really well.

"I do....." she answered trailing off.

"We have that signing and seminar at Crest Wood Bed and Breakfast and it's only an hour and a half from where Knox is playing in Stern."

"Oh!" she exclaimed turning quickly to grab her phone. "I'll get right on it!"

"Wait!" I chuckled. "Let's not let Knox in on this little fact, okay? I want to surprise him."

"Look at you, lover girl," she laughed. "We will make it a surprise he will never forget."

Chapter Six

*"Your heart knows what it wants regardless of your head,
distance is tossed out the window."*

"Good god girl! Slow down!" Meghan all but yelled in frustration.

I couldn't help it that my legs were longer than hers and that I might have been a little excited. Due to the weather and traffic we had arrived later than planned at the concert venue. Somehow I had managed to keep it from Knox during our conversations the last few times we had talked and Ace had been awesome in helping Meghan and I get set up with a room nearby for the night as well as backstage passes. I had battled with the decision of whether to show up too early because I didn't want to be a distraction, however, Ace assured me that I wouldn't be and, if anything, Knox would perform better knowing I was there.

Reaching behind me I found my friend's hand and pulled her along without slowing down. The first of two opening acts had already started playing, so I knew we had limited time to find Ace and Knox before he had to be on stage. As we got to an area swarming with people, I caught Cort out of the corner of my eye. Heading directly for him, with Meghan still in tow, my stomach started to turn in anticipation. Even though he was talking to someone else, Cort quickly flashed his smile when he saw us coming in his direction. Just before we reached him, I noticed the recognition dawn on him and the wattage behind his grin increase.

"Knox is going to flip!" he exclaimed gathering me into a bear hug when we got to him.

"Well, hello to you, too," I sputtered laughing. "I hope so!"

"Come!"

He excused himself from the man he had been talking to and took us down a hallway. Along the way, I explained I was surprising Knox and that Ace had helped us. Cort told us he was finishing up with a "Meet and Greet" session. He ushered us through a door and I was immediately unsure of my decision. We had entered from the side and Knox was standing in front of a promo screen taking pictures with some women. He couldn't see us and we couldn't see him, but the gaggle of women and girls lined up made me flinch.

I felt a jerk on my hand and turned slightly to find Meghan giving me an encouraging smile and trying to lead me to where Cort was now standing with Ace. My feet moved on their own accord. She squeezed my hand before releasing it and giving the tour manager a hug. He turned to me next and I moved into his arms for a quick hello.

"Take a breath," he whispered. "He will be so excited to see you."

I stepped back and gave him a wobbly smile. Normally, in this kind of situation, I wouldn't be nervous at all. I had done tons of book signings and talks in front of hundreds of people. However, I wasn't sure exactly how I was supposed to act. We hadn't discussed anything. Friends, that's how I would treat it, that I could do. I took Ace's advice and looking around I noticed the crowd starting to thin a bit. He took my hand and we started towards the screen where Knox was still obstructed from our view.

"Hey buddy," Ace greeted. "We have one more special lady that would like her picture taken with you."

I rolled my eyes and stepped up beside him. My breath caught in my throat. Knox had on a hunter green t-shirt, black fitted boot cut jeans, his worn black cowboy boots, and had topped it all off with one of his own black fitted baseball caps on backwards. My heart pounded and I felt my face immediately flush. Taking his time looking towards us, since he was signing a picture, I used the moment to compose myself. His head came up with a genuine smile, but when he saw it was me, his face lit up like a little boy at Christmas. The smile was contagious and I couldn't hold mine in.

"Special isn't a strong enough word," he retorted coming towards us and giving me a friendly hug.

It was probably a good thing the crowd was still lingering because I'm not sure what would have happened. I knew what I wanted to do, as did my lady parts, yet I wasn't completely sure about him. His hands lingered as we pulled from our hug and he used one hand on the small of my back to steer me back to the screen. He left one arm loose around my waist, however I felt his fingers on my bare skin where my shirt had ridden up from the top of my jeans. I put my arm around him and lopped a couple of fingers into his back pocket and tugged a bit causing him to chuckle.

The photographer took a couple pictures and when I pulled out of his embrace, I saw Knox call him over and say something. He sent a quick glance in my direction along with a smile and nodded. The horde of people had finally left the room, so Knox came back to where we were gathered. I saw a silent signal pass between Ace and Knox before we all started towards the door we had just come through with Cort.

"Please tell me you will be around after the show," came a whispered plea in my ear that sent tingles down my spine.

"In town for the night," I replied linking my hands in front of me so that I didn't give in to the urge to touch him.

"Thank God!" he exclaimed still whispering. "I need to put my hands on you."

I laughed, choked, and blushed all at the same time. Looking up at him was a mistake because his face held a shit-eating grin and he was casually adjusting his hat showing his bicep muscles off as his shirt sleeves rode up. I reddened even more and looked forward again so I didn't trip on my own feet, embarrassing me further. I felt his hand move to the small of my back once again as we got to the crowded space where we had originally met up with his brother. That's when I realized it was so packed because there wasn't anyone on stage except crew members moving instruments and microphones. It was almost time for Knox to go on.

The warmth on my back disappeared and when I turned to see where he had gone, I noticed the energy in the room shift. The excitement was starting to build and they weren't even on stage yet. Knox and his band had gathered in a circle, heads together and arms around each other. It didn't last more than 15-20 seconds, but it was moving to see the camaraderie. Once they separated, some went to the now darkened stage and Knox was hooked up to his ear piece and battery pack. I threw him a smile before letting Ace take Meghan and me off to the front of the stage where we could see the show. My heart was thudding along with the chanting crowd and I let myself be pulled into the anticipation of it all.

We hooted and hollered along with everyone else as the

remaining lights were turned down. The steady beat of the drums could be heard and slowly a guitar joined in. It was the opening cords for "Carnival" and by the time the lights came on the song was in full swing and Knox stood in the center of it all. His smile was ear-to-ear as he started on the first verse and it wasn't long before he ditched the mic stand to dance around the stage and interact with the crowd. He winked at us as he jumped into another song immediately after that was just as upbeat.

I couldn't believe his energy! He truly was in his element up there. The women continued to whistle and yell things, even when he was in between songs and just talking or grabbing a sip of water from the bottle behind him on the drum stands. I was floored by some of the comments and more than once I saw a bra go flying by us to land on the stage. One of the other members of the band would quickly remove it without a word. I had some pretty strong feelings for this man, but I completely understood how some women with husbands in the industry could feel insecure and jealous.

The lights dimmed again and Knox pulled the mic stand back out while Cort handed him his guitar. A light highlighted his position on the stage as he sat down on a stool and adjusted the mic so it was even with his mouth. He wanted his hands free so he could concentrate on his guitar. He plucked a few strings and through the dark I could see his brother setting up beside him with his own instrument. They were going to play an acoustic set together.

"So, we are going to slow it down for a couple songs for those love birds out there," Knox told them as he continued to tune his guitar. "This first one is from all the men out there to the special women in their lives."

As he started to sing "She's All Mine" his eyes closed and his baritone voice got deeper, if that was even possible. He seemed to get lost in the song and chills ran through me. When he got to the chorus he turned his head in our direction and our eyes locked. It felt like everyone else in the entire venue had disappeared and it was just us. By the time he moved his attention back to the crowd I was a pile of mush and literally had to lean into Meghan to steady myself.

The rest of the concert passed in a blur. Probably because I couldn't wait to spend some time with him that didn't include a computer or telephone screen between us. Once the encore was over and the lights came back on, Ace appeared at our side to take us backstage again. The noise and energy were both still on high as we reached the guys. I could only imagine how long it took for them to unwind after a show. I saw them knock back a couple of shots of whiskey together before they split and Knox headed our way.

"Shower and dinner?" he asked putting his hand on my back to steer me around people while we followed Ace and Meghan down a different hallway to the exit.

"Shower?" I asked in return my voice squeaking.

"Yes, for me," he grinned.

I blushed furiously and looked down. I swear my brain turned to Jell-O every time I was around him, or it just jumped in the gutter. Either way, I was constantly putting my foot in my mouth. He chuckled at my discomfort and moved his hand up to squeeze my shoulder. It didn't stay there long since we ended up being stopped by fans multiple times before we finally reached his tour bus.

Climbing aboard, he instantly excused himself to clean up while the three of us hung out in the spacious living room. My phone rang while we were waiting and noticing that it was my mother, I answered to make sure everything back home was all set. While I was talking to her I had gotten up and was leaning against the counter in the kitchenette. She was not an easy person to get off the phone once she was on. I saw Meghan and Ace head back off the bus when I was talking, but didn't think much of it.

At least not until I heard a noise signaling that Knox was done his shower and was headed back towards the front of the bus. I caught him out of the corner of my eye and started to tune my mother out. His hair was still damp from his shower and he was dressed in a green plaid button up shirt with faded blue jeans. Gone were the black cowboy boots, only to be replaced by just as worn brown work boots. His eyes were on me and I couldn't focus on the phone I still held to my ear.

"Sorry, mom," I stuttered. "What was that again?"

She answered me, yet I didn't hear a word she said because a certain singer had stopped in front of me and had placed his hands on the kitchen counter on either side of my hips effectively trapping me. His smell was intoxicating and his body was merely inches from mine. I closed my eyes taking in the close proximity of him and finally gave up on anything my poor mother was blabbing in my ear.

"I'll call you when we hit the road in the morning," I told her, cutting her off and hitting the button on my screen before she even had time to finish her sentence.

"You didn't need to do that."

"Kind of hard to concentrate with you that close," I informed him placing my cell phone behind me and putting my hands next to his.

"I told you I couldn't wait to get my hands on you. I wasn't kidding."

Before I could reply, his mouth came crashing down on mine and his hands came down on my hips pulling me flush against his hard body. I gasped in surprise and as my hands came up to his chest to steady myself, he dove his tongue into my mouth. I met him stroke for stroke and moaned when I felt his erection against my belly. The invitation was all he needed to roll his hips against mine, much like I had seen him do on stage, and one of his hands slid down to cup my ass. I moved my hands up to wrap around his neck and couldn't resist tangling my fingers into his hair.

KNOCK! KNOCK!

"Hey you two! Stop necking! Some of us are hungry!"

We pulled apart panting and he rested his forehead against mine. Catching our breath for a moment, he finally pulled away and adjusted himself. I couldn't help it and a giggle escaped me. He looked so darn uncomfortable.

"I am so glad you're here," he said kissing me one more time before taking my hand in his and pulling me towards the door of the bus.

The four of us went to a little diner down the street from where the concert was. Either Ace had called ahead and cleared the place out or they weren't busy this time of night because we were the only ones in there. Not that that lasted long, part of the band soon joined us. Though I would have liked the one-on-one time with Knox, it was great to see and meet them all. The laughs were well worth it as well. The stories had tears streaming down my face and Meghan had snorted more times than I could count while we were with them. I was pretty sure my abs had gotten the workout of a lifetime.

"Have I told you how happy I am that you are here?" he asked leaning in to whisper in my ear as the others continued to chat around us.

"Only a few hundred times," I replied snuggling into his side and putting my head against the arm he had resting on the back of the booth seat.

Using his free hand, he brushed a stray hair from my face. Then, cupping my cheek, he ran his thumb across my lips. His eyes were warm and filled with something I couldn't quite put my finger on. Here we were just a man and a woman, there was no paparazzi, no famous singer, no successful author. Just us and his family and friends. He bent down and kissed me softly before pulling me closer to him with the arm that was around me.

Several hours later when I was stifling a yawn, I looked up at the clock on the wall. I blinked hard to make sure I had read it right and sure enough it said two o'clock. As in a.m.!! No wonder I was dragging. I had been up for almost 24 hours between my book signing and the concert. I curled into Knox's side and inhaled his scent. The smell that was his and his alone.

The guys all started getting up and heading out the door. Everyone had finally wound down from the show and exhaustion was setting in. Before we stepped outside the door, he pulled me in for one final hug and a long deep kiss. Once we stepped back onto the street we would go back to doing the secret dating thing again, not that I was complaining. I understood and I was fine with it.

"This is the part that I hate and that is just going to keep getting harder, leaving you," he stated still holding me against him.

"It does, but it only makes us stronger," I told him squeezing one last time before I shifted back, afraid I wouldn't let go if I didn't at that moment.

Ace took Meghan and I back to the hotel, just like he had in Nashville, and Cort and Knox had headed back to the bus. After getting into our pajamas and performing our nightly rituals, we literally fell into bed. My friend was out within seconds, but despite being so overtired, sleep eluded me. My phone vibrated beside me and I grabbed it before it woke her up.

Miss you in my arms already <3

The tears started to fall, only this time they weren't happy ones. This man had so quickly captured my heart. It was going to be a battle to have a relationship with him, of that I was sure. However, as I looked at the selfie we had taken on my phone and how right it felt to be in his arms, I knew it would all work out.

Chapter Seven

"Love is not planned nor is it tied up in a neat little package, it is messy and it is exhilarating."

"You need to eat," Meghan pushed as she put a plate of finger food on the corner of my desk.

I waved her off and kept on typing. My writing came in waves. There were times when the proverbial block would be so bad that I couldn't put anything down on paper for weeks, or it would flow so freely that eating and sleeping weren't even options. Today, yesterday, and the day before, I think, the words were all but writing themselves. My hands couldn't seem to keep up with what was coming out of my brain. I continued on, ignoring the food and my annoyed friend who I could see out of the corner of my eye. When it looked like she wasn't going away, I finished the chapter and pushed myself back from my desk. Pinching the bridge of my nose, I closed my eyes and took a deep breath to clear my head.

"What's up?" I finally asked looking up at her, and that's when I saw it, the worry. "I'm sorry."

I stood up and wrapped my arms around her. I forgot that my friends never saw me when I got like this. Normally, I would fall off the radar for a bit and my family would take care of the animals. Then I would reconnect with the girls like nothing had ever happened. While I was hugging her I heard noise from downstairs. Pulling away, I left my hands on her shoulders and gave her a questioning look.

"I may have called in reinforcements," she said shrugging and ducking out of my reach to grab the plate with the food on it.

I sighed and moved back to my computer to save the file I had been working on. That's when I caught a whiff of myself. I knew that I had been tied up for a few days, but I hadn't realized how long it had been since I had had a shower. Instead of following Meghan downstairs, I detoured to my bedroom and the master bath so I could clean up. Twenty minutes later in a long-sleeved t-shirt and yoga pants I went down to see my friends.

All three girls were sprawled in various spots in the living room. Two serving platters of finger foods were on the coffee table and each lady held either a glass of wine or beer. As soon as they saw me, Kelly jumped up and went to the kitchen motioning for me to sit. I plopped down in the empty recliner. She returned carrying a frosted mug of my favorite beer at the same time Alicia handed me a plate full of food and a napkin.

"You ladies are so good to me," I told them as I stuffed my face, suddenly realizing I was extremely hungry.

"So, do you always do this?" Alicia asked, concern all over her face.

"Yeah, I'm sorry," I apologized taking another sip of my drink and putting my empty plate on the table beside my chair. "I write in waves. When it comes it comes, so I usually send a message to my mother and they help with the boys. It will last a few days and it normally takes a day or so for me to recover physically."

"Did I mess with it by pulling you away?" Meghan questioned biting her lip.

"No," I assured her with a smile. "The story is still running in my brain, just quieter than it has been the past few days."

"What triggers it?" Kelly wanted to know.

"I'm not sure exactly," I answered honestly. "However, I haven't written like that or wanted to write like that since Brandon and I split."

"Knox," all three of them said at once.

"Knox? What about him?"

"He's the reason you have been able to write," Meghan pointed out.

Before I could respond I heard my phone going off, Meghan obviously had made sure it was charged and had brought it down. It sat on the coffee table with the others and I hesitated to answer it since they were all piled together. Alicia pulled it from the group and once she saw the screen she handed it to me with a grin. It was an alert for a FaceTime session with none other than the man we had been talking about. When I swiped my finger across the screen his gorgeous bearded face filled it.

"Welcome back to earth, beautiful," he greeted.

"Hey handsome, did you just finish a show?"

"Still a little disoriented, huh? Yeah, good show, amazing crowd."

"Awesome. Do you mind if I let you go and FaceTime you in a bit? The girls are here."

"Not a problem...."

"Don't you dare hang up on that poor good-looking man," Alicia chided me and when I looked up I figured out why.

The girls had filled my plate and my beer one more time

and left them on the coffee table. Everything else had been taken care of and they were all bundled up in their jackets. I raised my eyebrows at them and at Knox laughing quietly on my phone. They all laughed as well and hugged me before traipsing out the front door.

"What was that about?"

"I may have had Ace call Meghan when I hadn't heard from you for a few days."

"I'm sorry. I guess I didn't realize how little everyone knew about my writing process."

"Don't worry about it," he assured me as he shifted on his bed to get comfortable. "Where did we leave off last time? Oh, last relationship?"

"Oy," I let out as I took a long sip of beer. "Ended seven months ago. It was a five-year relationship, though I am pretty sure it was over long before we officially ended it. His name was Brandon and he cheated on me with a woman we both know."

"Ouch."

"Oh, it gets better. He got her pregnant."

"Double ouch."

"Not done," I said as I picked up a couple of cracker and cheese sandwiches from my plate. "He is my brother, Matt's best friend, and has been since we were kids. He really is a decent guy. I'm not sure what happened."

"And you still kissed me? Wow! You should pretty much hate men right now. That man is a freaking idiot."

I smiled at him and finished the rest of the snacks on my plate. We were quiet for a minute as I drained my beer as well. When I thought back to my relationship with Brandon, I had been the idiot. I should have listened to my brother and never gone out with him. I'm not exactly sure how we lasted as long as we did anyway. By the end, we were just roommates and had barely hung on to the friendship we had started with.

"Your turn. Last relationship?"

"A year ago. I made a try at it with a woman from back home, someone I thought I knew. She started getting jealous of all the women around me. Her name was Angela. She became clingy and wanted to tour with me. Come to find out all she wanted was the fame, not me."

"And you think I shouldn't like men? Pretty sure women like that give the rest of us a bad name."

"You aren't like her," he stated matter-of-factly while he flashed me one of his smiles that teased of his dimple.

"Oh? How can you be so sure?"

"Multiple things. You wouldn't have surprised me a few weeks ago or kept up the friend façade in front of everyone. You also would have freaked that first night I met you when I saved you from the drunk."

"Speaking of friend façade," I started slowly, it was now or never. "What exactly are we? How do you want me to act?"

"Well...I would like to think we are dating," he answered, his cheeks turning a slight shade of pink under his beard.

"Sounds perfect to me," I replied feeling my own cheeks get warm.

"As for how we are supposed to act, you probably won't like this."

He grew quiet and started running his fingers through his hair. What I would give to be having this conversation in person so I could touch him and comfort him. I understood his concerns on all levels, especially with what he had just told me about his ex-girlfriend. I gave him an encouraging smile and gestured for him to go ahead.

"I would like to keep this out of the spotlight for now," he explained. "I want to know that if it doesn't work it is because of us and not outside forces."

"Are you sure you can't pinch me?" I asked him.

He laughed and it broke the seriousness of the conversation. It was then I realized how exhausted I was. The past three days suddenly came crashing down on me. Knox must have noticed because he asked what I needed to do before bed. I still had to go out to the barn to check on the horses and I told him so. He told me to keep him on FaceTime and take the phone with me. Giving him a strange look, I headed to the kitchen, donned my winter jacket and boots, and snapped on the outside light.

"So, why do you want to do night check with me?" I questioned as I made my way out the glass sliders and across the crunchy frost covered lawn to the barn.

"It's not that I want to do night check with you," he informed me, "it's that I want to tuck you in. Just like I do every night that we talk."

Tears instantly pricked the backs of my eyes and I had to turn the phone away for a second. I wouldn't deny I was a beautiful woman or that I had had a wonderful childhood, but damn if I knew how I had gotten lucky enough to meet this man and have him fall for me. This long-distance thing was definitely going to be tricky. When he made comments like that all I wanted to do was be wrapped in his arms.

Taking a deep breath, I brought the phone back up and opened the door into the tack room with my free hand. Hitting the light switch I grabbed a handful of peppermint treats from the bin by the door and continued through the room to the door separating it from the inside of the rest of the barn. The minute I turned on the light inside the main barn I heard the boys shuffling around and heads popped over their half doors. Nickers soon followed.

"Are you going to introduce me?" Knox asked as I moved toward the stalls.

Laughing, I did just that. I let myself into each stall and while the boys munched on their treats I would tell Knox their stories. I told him about how Max had been my present for high school graduation, that Gem had come from a family friend going through a divorce, and how Case had simply stolen my heart from a rescue site. They were all very special and meant the world to me. Double checking that they were all locked up again, I dropped kisses on each of their velvety noses and went back out the way I had come.

Knox filled my trek back inside with a story from their show that night, and how everything Cort seemed to touch would fall apart or break. His voice was soothing and I enjoyed listening to his life away from me. Especially those stories that included his brother. I loved that he had such close relationships with his family members despite his crazy schedule.

He continued about almost falling flat on his face while I removed my boots and jacket, and locked up the house for the night. How he still had energy was beyond me. I tried to concentrate on his stories as I dragged myself up the stairs and into my bedroom, but I had officially hit a wall physically. Not bothering to hit any switches, I used my phone to light my way to my bed. I crawled under the covers and snuggled in with a sigh.

"You're toast, huh baby?"

"Yep."

"Okay. I've done my job anyway. I tucked you in."

"Thank you," I mumbled reaching up to grab the cord for my cell phone.

"You're welcome," he replied crawling under the covers himself. "Now get some sleep. We will catch up tomorrow."

"Night handsome."

"Night beautiful."

The next morning, I woke up disoriented and in a panic. I laid still for a moment trying to figure out what exactly woke me up. That's when I heard it, CLANG. I sat straight up. Someone was in my house. I turned to grab my cell phone, but it was gone. The minute I saw that and caught a whiff of something cooking, I knew it was my mother. She had taken my phone to let me sleep in because she didn't know how to turn the ringer off and I always forgot.

Dashing to the bathroom, I did my business and put a brush through my hair before pulling it up into a messy bun. I ran down the stairs, like a little kid, so excited to see my mom. When I got to the doorway she had her back to me flipping pancakes on my griddle. Her hair was pulled back much like mine and she was dressed in worn jeans and a hooded sweatshirt. Barn boots and a jacket were next to mine near the sliding doors, so I could only guess she had already fed the boys outside. I made my way to the bar and plopped myself down into the closest chair.

"About time you joined the real world," she joked turning around and putting a coffee cup in front of me.

"Thank you for taking care of my kids," I replied rolling my eyes slightly and grinning at her.

"Couldn't let them starve," she stated with a chuckle as she expertly flipped the pancakes onto two plates and turning off the griddle.

The jesting was always the same. She would give me a hard time about neglecting my animals when she secretly loved taking care of them, and about being absent from the everyday world. Once the joking was done she would get down to asking about other things in life. She was my mother, but also my friend. We had always had a close relationship.

"So, how is the book coming along?" she asked as she sat down next to me with the remaining condiments.

"Good. Plot line is flowing really well and the characters are basically creating themselves," I told her while I covered my pancakes generously with maple syrup.

"You haven't been this enthusiastic about writing in quite some time," she observed.

I shook my head since I had a mouth full of food. It was true. I had always enjoyed what I did, I wouldn't have gotten where I was otherwise. However, the drive I had to be at my computer had been wavering until recently. My mom would know since she did all my pre-editing before I sent it to my actual editor and publisher. One of the benefits to having a mother that used to be an English/Lit Professor at a college nearby.

"I'm hoping to have the first half of the book to you by next week," I informed her when I finally came up for air.

"Perfect. Next week is quiet."

"I swear, you are busier now than you were when you were actually working," I ribbed her, finishing up my pancakes.

"That's because I'm busy helping you all the time," she shot back lightly, picking up our plates and taking them to the sink.

I stuck my tongue out at her good naturedly and nursed the remainder of my coffee. Before resetting my Keurig she slid a pile of mail over to me, including a small package. I made quick work of the bills and junk mail. I was about to open the small box when my mom joined me again with fresh cups of coffee for both of us and a question that had me going still.

"So, when are you going to tell me about this boy?"

"First of all, I'm pretty sure I started dating men when I was in my 20s. Secondly, where did you hear I was dating someone?"

"Kelly mentioned it at dinner the other night."

"Of course she did," I muttered, one of the downfalls to one of my good friends being my future sister-in-law was that she often told my parents things before I had a chance. "It's complicated."

"The distance?" she pushed.

"Did she tell you who it was?" I asked starting to open the package.

"All she said was that you met someone in Nashville that you were dating online and over the phone."

"You wouldn't believe me if I told you," I replied honestly as I pulled opened the flaps.

She might have commented, but my concentration was solely on the picture staring back at me. It was a 5x7 of Knox and I, the one the professional photographer had taken at the concert. Other than the fact that his hand was on my bare skin, it looked like any other Meet and Greet picture of fan and artist. I set the picture aside, putting it between us on the counter.

Next was a note from Knox:

Thought you might like the first one. I know it's a night I will never forget, but this next one is the one that reminds me why I saved you from that drunk in Nashville. So I could have a chance with a gorgeous woman that makes me feel like the only man in the room.

<3

Knox

Moving the paper aside I instantly covered my mouth and had to fight back the tears that filled my eyes. At the bottom of the box was a 4x6 of the two of us from the diner. It was when I had leaned my head against his arm and he had brushed the hair out of my face. Obviously Meghan or Ace had snapped it on one of their phones.

"This is why it's complicated," I whispered handing her the second picture.

"I don't understand," she said, her eyes misty and soft.

"Because I'm falling in love with him."

Chapter Eight

"The laughter from those you care about can warm the soul, the vibrations like a fire on a cold winter's night."

Thanksgiving had come and gone and I was getting antsy to see Knox again. It was a good thing I had a few small signings and talks before Christmas, they were great distractions. His tour and traveling had picked up, so unfortunately between that and my erratic need to write, we had had little chance to even connect on FaceTime. The texts were slowing as well, though we did try to send at least one a day. If only Meghan could work her magic on Ace so we could see each other.

"I'm sorry, bud," I told Case as I patted him on the rump. "I know I am mildly distracted."

I had spent a better part of the morning trying to write, but it just wouldn't flow as well as it had been. I had finally given up and Meghan and I had used the time to organize for the signings that weekend and the following. Christmas was a great time to sell and meet new people. We had called it quits at lunch time and I figured I would spend the afternoon cleaning the barn and giving the boys some much needed attention.

"Okay, last foot," I murmured as I ran my hand down his leg to signal him to pick it up.

Case was a joy to work around and responded immediately. I went to work on cleaning his hoof out and checking it for any bruises or stones that might have been stuck. He nickered while I was cleaning and I spoke to him in response. The horse had always been a "talker." I set his foot down gently when I was done, gave him one last pat, and turned towards his head. That's when I realized I wasn't alone.

The nickers from the horse hadn't been for me, but for the person that had come into the barn. Standing at Case's head patting his face gently was Knox, or at least I thought it was him. He was dressed in dark wash jeans, work boots, a hooded sweatshirt, and a jacket. His hair was windblown and begged for me to run my fingers through it. I rubbed my eyes multiple times as I returned the hoof pick to my brush box. I wanted to make sure I wasn't dreaming.

"You can rub them all you want," he said ducking under the cross tie attached to Case's halter. "I'm not going to disappear though."

I jumped into his arms as soon as he was close enough and hugged him for all I was worth. The smell, the feel, the heat, it was all him. His arms circled me and held tight. I could feel his breath in my hair and I sighed. I never wanted to move.

"Don't pinch me this time, okay?" I whispered. "If it's a dream, I don't want to wake up."

With my comment, Knox pulled away enough to cup my face with his hands. He brushed his lips across mine sweetly a couple of times and his eyes remained locked on mine. My hands flexed against his jacket at his waist. I could get lost in those eyes, that mouth.

"Baby, this isn't a dream. For the next two days, I'm all yours."

"Really?!"

"Yep, I rented a room in Ander and a vehicle."

"A room?" I asked raising my eyebrows. "I think not. I have plenty of room, you will stay with me."

"Are you sure?"

"Yes. Let me put Case away and we can go up to the house and get you settled in."

He stood back and leaned against the wall with an uncertain look on his face. I unhooked my horse from his cross ties and turned him around. Unlatching the gate, I maneuvered him outside, without letting the other two in, and shut it. I pulled down the overhead door and grabbed my brush box with one hand. When I looked up to reach for Knox's hand with my other, I found him watching me with a soft smile on his face. I raised my eyebrows at him in question.

"You are so comfortable with them, so in love with them," he said in awe.

"They are my kids," I replied simply, threading my fingers through his and tugging him towards the tack room.

Once my box was taken care of, we headed to the house. He pulled away to jog to his truck to grab his bag and while he did that I eyed the sky. They were calling for a storm tonight to bring us between six and eight inches of snow and the clouds were starting to roll in. When we met at the sliding glass door, he gave me a kiss on the nose and opened it for me. Stepping inside I slipped off my boots and jacket.

"When I go out to the barn I use this door, the rest of the time I use the front. You can leave your boots wherever," I told him getting out of his way.

"Shower?" he asked once he had his boots off and his jacket was hung up with mine.

"Bathroom is down the hall to the right, linens are in the closet," I said feeling my face instantly turn red.

Chuckling, Knox came over and gave me a quick kiss before heading down the hall with this bag. Knowing I had to keep my hands busy or I would go crazy, I pulled a homemade lasagna from the freezer and turned the oven on to preheat. With that done I took the makings for a salad out and got to work. It was closing in on five o'clock when I put the lasagna in the oven and set the timer. It would be ready by six, which gave me time to catch the news and get the boys in. That left me the rest of the night to relax with Knox. Smiling to myself I spun to head out of the kitchen and bumped into a solid wall of man.

"Well, hello there pretty lady."

"Hi," I greeted shyly as he backed me into the counter.

"I don't think we got a proper hello earlier," he told me, leaning down and nibbling my lower lip.

"Oh?" I uttered on a sigh as my hands slid up his chest to wrap around his neck.

That was all the invitation he needed before his mouth came down on mine, insistent and hot. His hands tugged on my sweatshirt and t-shirt before I felt them on my skin. He ran them up my back and chills ran through me causing me to moan into his mouth. Bringing them back down, he gripped my waist and pulled me flush against him. My hips tipped up on their own and his erection shifted in his jeans. This time the moan came from him. His lips left mine and made a trail across my cheek and down my neck.

The feeling of his beard on my neck and collarbone sent all the blood pooling to my clit. A throaty groan came from me that I had never heard before. My noise had him grinding his pelvis into mine and I thought for a second I would orgasm just from his mouth and hands on me despite the fact that I was fully clothed. Seconds later his ministrations ceased and he rested his head on my shoulder. My arms slipped from around his neck and I settled them on his waist as we caught our breaths.

"Wow."

"I was thinking the same thing," he said as he lifted his head and looked me in the eyes. "I gave you whisker burn."

"That's the least of my problems," I replied smirking and shifting my hips.

He laughed and dropped a kiss on my nose while he cupped my face in his hands. Before he could bring his lips back to mine I heard the tell-tale exhaust of my brother's truck. I brought my head down to Knox's chest and took a couple of deep breaths. I knew why he was here, he always checked on me right before a snow storm. However, I was worried about how he would react to my company.

"Are you ready to meet my brother?" I asked, bringing my head back up to look at him as I heard the truck shut off.

"Are *you* ready for me to meet your brother?"

I nodded, but neither of us moved from being wrapped in each other's arms. The front door opened and there were two voices in the house. When the door shut and they started down the hall towards us I knew exactly who was with him. I cringed internally. Brandon came into the kitchen first and around Knox's shoulder I saw a dozen emotions roll across his face.

"Hey guys," I greeted, coming out from around my man.

"Hi," Matt finally spoke up. "I didn't realize you had company."

"Surprise visit," I told him leaning against the bar. "Matt, Brandon, this is Knox. Knox, my brother, Matt, and his friend Brandon."

Knox moved around me to offer his hand to the guys and put his free hand on the small of my back. The tension in the room was thick. Minus my father, these were the most important men in my life. They had better learn to get along.

"So, Matt, what can I do for you?" I questioned leaning into Knox's hand, even though I knew the reason they had stopped.

"Just checking in before the storm," he stated moving to stand by the kitchen table. "You all set driving in this stuff?" he directed at Knox.

"I am," he replied easily.

I applauded him for not rising to my brother's bait and I gave Matt a look to back off. Brandon stood near the doorway looking like he wanted to turn and run. This just needed to end. I wanted my quiet time with my man, especially since it was limited.

"Well, we're good, as you can see," I informed him, "so why don't you guys head out so we can go take care of the boys."

"Take Brandon out to help you," he gestured towards his friend. "I want to have a little talk with your man here."

I took a step towards my brother. I was seething. I felt strong arms lock around my waist and a solid chest at my back. I leaned into him and took a deep breath to calm myself down. Matt never acted like this, I couldn't believe him. I turned around and looked into warm brown eyes. His smile was enough to let me know he was fine with it, even though I wasn't. He gave me a quick kiss and turned me with a light shove towards the sliding glass doors.

I slid on my boots and grabbed my jacket, all without saying a word. The look on my face had my brother ducking his head and heading to the refrigerator. Brandon came up behind me and opened the door for me. I scooted out ahead of him and made my way to the barn. Snowflakes danced around me. Normally I would laugh and dance with them, but tonight I was angry and confused and frustrated. Brandon grabbed the barn door and opened it for me. I smiled at him, relaxing a bit. I had forgotten what a gentleman he was.

"I'm sorry," I apologized as we started preparing the grain for the horses.

"For what?"

"For my attitude," I replied setting down the bucket I was working on. "I'm just floored about Matt."

"That's probably partly my fault," he admitted putting his bucket down as well. "When we split up he was angry with me. We had it out more than once."

I finished the last bucket and stood back to look at him. I hadn't realized that he and Matt had had any problems when we had gone our separate ways. They had been friends for as long as I could remember, they were as close as brothers. I took him in as he told me everything. He was the exact opposite of Knox in every way physically. He was muscular, yet thin with blonde hair and startling green eyes. The thing that I really noticed now, after all these years, was that his smile was slower to come than the man I was currently with. I wondered why that was.

"I get that he is being the protective big brother," I told him as we made our way into the main barn to place buckets in stalls. "However, this is still so new and complicated. I don't want him to scare him away before I get a chance to see where it is really going."

"You don't need to worry about your brother scaring Knox away," he said opening the overhead door.

He paused to pat each nose before unlatching the gate to let them in. I watched him as he moved around them to make sure they were all locked in their stalls after they had gone into the correct ones. I had missed this, our companionship. Not our relationship, but the friendship we had shared for so many years before that.

"So tell me, why don't I have to worry about my brother?" I

wanted to know as we took empty buckets out of the stalls and locked them up once again.

"That man is in love with you."

I stopped in my tracks on my way back to the tack room and looked at him with wide eyes. He nudged me to keep moving and we put everything away. Before we walked out of the room he blocked my way and put his hands on my shoulders. I looked into his eyes and saw the friend there that I had had since I was a young girl.

"He looks at you the same way I look at Emmy. Like there is no one else in the room, like he would fight to the end of the world for you, like you were made for him."

Tears pricked my eyes. I allowed him to wrap me in his arms briefly for a hug before wiping my eyes and heading out of the barn and towards the house. We changed the conversation to lighter things on our walk through the snow. I stopped on the porch and looked at him, not sure if I should go in or not. He gave my hand a squeeze and opened the door for me. I stepped into my kitchen and was not prepared for what I found.

Knox sat with this back to me at the kitchen table with this long legs out in front of him and crossed. He was laughing at a story my brother was telling him about us as children and had a beer resting in his hands. My brother was on the other side of the table in much the same position. His blue eyes met mine and he nodded at me with an "I'm sorry" smile. I took my boots off and handed my jacket to Brandon for him to hang up before going to Matt and planting a kiss on the top of his head. He patted my leg and he and Brandon immediately started in on another story.

I grabbed them all fresh beers from the refrigerator and brought them back to them at the table. When I handed Knox his, he grabbed my hand and kissed the back of it. I melted with his smile and leaned over to kiss him on the cheek. Smiling, I turned and headed back to the kitchen. I was in a hot chocolate mood, so I set the machine and went about finishing up with dinner. Pulling out the lasagna I set it on the stove to cool while I put the garlic bread in for a few minutes to warm. I sipped from my cup and couldn't wipe the happy expression from my face as I listened to the men chatter behind me. It didn't get much better than this.

My brother and Brandon ended up staying for dinner and on their way out, checked on the boys. The storm was starting to pick up intensity by the time they left so I made them both promise to text me when they got to their respective homes. It was already nine o'clock when we finished cleaning up the kitchen and I could tell Knox was dead on his feet. Silently, I locked the back door and took his hand in mine to lead him down the hallway. He pulled me to a stop in front of the guest bedroom and tilted his head. I leaned down to grab the bag that he had left there and tugged his hand to get him moving again.

"I can sleep down here," he assured me, standing his ground and causing me to bounce back into him so that we were almost nose to nose.

"I want you in my bed, beside me, holding me," I responded squeezing his hand. "I'm not going to lie, I'm not ready for sex yet, but I need you next to me."

That was all he needed. He took his bag from my hand and kissed me gently on the lips before leading me the rest of the way down the hall and around to the stairs. He followed me up and into my bedroom. I moved to the bathroom to brush my teeth and change my clothes. When I returned in my cami and shorts, he was in bed in his boxer briefs with the comforter and sheets turned down waiting for me. I stood for a moment and looked him over blatantly. He was a gorgeous man, inside and out. He was solid and husky, yet I didn't see an ounce of fat on him. His chest was sprinkled with hair the same color as that on his head and it lead down his stomach to a v pointing at his manhood that was straining against the tight black fabric encasing it. When my eyes found his he had a shit-eating grin on his face.

Smirking, I climbed in and snuggled into his side as he covered us up. His body was warm against mine and I felt my nipples and clit respond to being so close to him and having our legs twined together. He rubbed one hand up and down my side over my shirt and the other rested on the pillow under my head. I ran my hand up his arm and watched as his muscles danced under my fingers. His eyes were closed when I looked back up at his face and his hand was starting to slow in its movements. The traveling was catching up with him.

I rested my hand on his bare chest and felt his heart beating steadily beneath it. Even though my body was ready for the next step with him, my heart and head were not. I had only been with two men in my life, Brandon being one of them, and I didn't want to rush things with Knox. This man was everything I had ever dreamed of and I had never felt like this before. I wanted to build something solid with him and hold on forever.

Chapter Nine

"Christmas presents from the heart are the best,
Those are the ones locked in your memory forever."

"I absolutely *love* your books," gushed a lady, old enough to be my grandmother, as I signed my latest novel for her.

"I'm so glad you enjoy them," I responded honestly.

The woman continued her chatter to her friend beside her as I handed the book back. Before they moved out of line she slipped me her grandson's phone number, telling me how perfect I would be for him and how beautiful I was. I thanked her and chuckled as she stepped aside to let the next person come ahead. I turned to give the paper to Meghan, who looked at me with wide eyes of disbelief.

An hour later, we took a break for lunch and left the bookstore. A small sandwich shop was just up the street and because it was such a bright, clear day we decided to walk. Snow on the sidewalks crunched under our feet and the sun was warm on my face. I hummed a little tune as we navigated our way since Meghan was on her cell phone.

"Okay, are your signings always like that?" she asked when she finally finished her call.

"Like what?" I responded, opening the door to the sandwich shop. "The never-ending lines? No, just around Christmas."

"No, the grandmothers, mothers, sisters, all giving you guys' numbers," she stammered, pulling the door shut behind us.

We got in line and both grabbed Thanksgiving wraps and hot chocolates. The place was still quiet, so it wasn't difficult to find a table. I knew she would start the conversation up again once we were settled. It happened, it had happened almost from the beginning. I just contributed it to my age and good looks, it wasn't a big deal.

"So, seriously? Does that always happen?"

"Yeah," I replied shrugging. "I've even had a grandmother drag her poor grandson to a signing to meet me."

"Oh geez," she muttered. "You are like the female version of Knox."

I stopped chewing and stared at her. Oh boy. To a degree she was right. Women and girls were constantly throwing themselves at him, between clothes and phone numbers. The only difference was that my fans were a little more subtle about it. Sighing, I finished what was in my mouth and had to nod my head in agreement.

"How are things going with the cowboy?" she asked as she took another bite of her sandwich.

Despite us working side-by-side every day, we didn't talk about personal stuff all that much. I had found out that she had helped Ace to get Knox here a few weeks ago when he had surprised me, which made complete sense when she didn't show up at all while he was at my house without my even texting her. I owed her big for that.

"Good," I told her when I finished a sip of my hot chocolate. "It's hard being apart, but it seems to be going well."

"Heard Brandon and Matt got to meet him."

"Damn Kelly and her big mouth!"

I filled her in on everything while we finished our meal. By the time we were headed back to the bookstore she was laughing so hard tears were streaming down her face. I rolled my eyes, yet I couldn't help but laugh with her. It would definitely be a story we could tell our children someday.

That night as I lay in bed waiting to FaceTime with Knox and working on my book, I winced knowing I needed to say something about the telephone numbers. It wasn't like it was a secret, but I wanted to be the one to tell him. Sighing, I leaned back against my pillows. Seconds later my phone chimed signaling a session. Swiping my screen, I was met with a very distraught looking man.

"Hey handsome," I greeted, "what's up?"

"Hey," he retorted running his hand through his hair for what looked to be the millionth time.

"Knox, what's wrong?" I asked sitting up straighter, he was beginning to worry me.

"There's something I need to tell you," he started as he moved around, clearly tonight they had rented hotel rooms. "Something I should have told you in person."

I felt all the blood leave my face. This was it. He didn't want to see me anymore. My heart started to ache in my chest. I took a deep breath and fought to keep my voice even and the tears at bay.

"Did you meet someone else?"

"What?!" he stammered.

"It's okay," I told him, surprisingly calm for the butterflies wreaking havoc with my stomach. "I understand."

"Woah! Woah! Woah!" he said raising his voice and putting his free hand up. "Baby, I didn't meet anyone. Even if I did, they wouldn't hold a candle to you."

I released the breath I had been holding and along with it came the tears. I tried to wipe them off before he saw them, however, I wasn't quick enough. I saw the sadness in his face and he once again ran his hand through his hair. I turned the phone long enough to mop up the mess with a tissue or two, took some deep breaths and faced him again.

"I knew I should have told you when I was there. Okay, here it is...Rebecca Hall is joining us on tour," he spit out. "And our duet on my new album? We are going to perform that during our shows."

"That's it?" I asked dumbfounded. "That's what you were stressing about?"

"That's it?!" he exclaimed. "Do you know what the assumptions will be despite the fact that she is happily married?!"

"I'm not too worried about what people say," I told him settling back in. "You don't owe me any explanations."

"Woman, you are going to be the death of me," he growled. "You are my girlfriend. You should demand explanations."

"I'm your girlfriend?" I squeaked. My eyes had widened with that comment. When had that happened? Did I miss something?

Knox froze. All his movements stopped and I saw him sit on the edge of the bed. His cheeks grew pink under his beard and his eyes went soft. The stress that had marred his face mere moments before, melted away.

"To me, you've been my girlfriend since the night you surprised me at the concert. Is that okay with you?"

"Yep," I replied gulping.

"I'm sorry I was so fired up. I'm nervous about the stories that will come out. I don't want to lose you before I get to really have you."

"I'm not going anywhere, cowboy," I said giving him a reassuring smile. "I trust you."

Those words had him closing his eyes and releasing a slow steady breath. He seemed to take the time to relax every muscle in his body. I never thought that he would worry about the press. Then again, it made sense, he was a fairly private person. He had obviously done a good job of keeping himself out of the negative part of the limelight up until now.

"Have I ever told you how lucky I was to have met you? Not many women would be as understanding."

"Well, I kinda know how you feel," I told him running my hand through my own hair. "I may have gotten ten numbers today at the signing."

"Ten numbers? As in telephone numbers?"

"Yeah, grandmothers, mothers, sisters. They all love me and give me telephone numbers for the single men in their lives."

"I don't know if I should be pissed at you for taking them or elated that I have such a hot woman," he teased.

The tense part of the conversation seemed to be past us and the rest centered mostly on the upcoming holiday. Knox and Cort were going to be able to spend Christmas Eve and Christmas Day with their family and he was very excited about it. All seemed to be well until I got ready to say goodnight and his last comment almost broke my heart.

"I want you for Christmas," he whispered.

Those five words had me texting both my mother and Ace the moment we were off the phone. Ace immediately responded and we put the wheels in motion. If I could do so without causing a huge ruckus within my family, I would be giving Knox exactly what he asked for. How could I deny that request from the man that I loved?

The answer was, I couldn't, and I was getting way too good at keeping secrets. A week and a half later, I was sitting on a plane taxiing into the airport in Nashville at four a.m. on Christmas Eve. My mother had been completely supportive while my brother and father had been a little more reserved. My body shook from head to toe, nerves or the weather I'm not sure which. I had never been away from my family for the holidays and I was going to be meeting Knox's to boot.

It seemed like forever before we were allowed off the plane. Finally, the captain gave us the okay and the few of us on the flight filtered out. Grabbing my jacket and my overly large carry-on, I got off the plane and headed towards the baggage claim. Even though I didn't actually have any other bags, we figured it was the easiest place to meet. Ace was supposed to be my ride, but that was not the person I found waiting for me.

"Cort?"

"Hey gorgeous!" he greeted enveloping me into a bear hug.

"Hi!" I replied squeezing him tightly in return. "Everything okay with Ace?"

"Yep. He told me the plan and I asked if I could come get you. I can't wait to see my brother's face!"

I smiled at him and handed him my bag at his request. Following him out to the parking lot and his truck, I took him in. He wasn't quite as solid as Knox, but was just as fit. His hair was the same brown tone, yet he wore his longer so it barely brushed his shoulders. Cort and his brother shared the same warm brown eyes as well, though his face was clean shaven.

"Flight was good?" he asked as we settled in to the truck.

"As good as a red eye can be," I chuckled.

"You probably would like to clean up," he commented, pulling out of the parking lot. "And need coffee."

"Double yes!"

"We have an apartment here in town," he informed me as we drove. "You can shower there before we head to my parents and we'll grab coffee on the way."

"Perfect."

Moments later we were pulling into a small parking lot at the back of a brick building. When I looked a little closer I recognized it as the bar we had met the guys at that night during our vacation, Cash's. I glanced over at Cort confused and he smiled and motioned for me to follow him. I jumped out of the truck and noticed that there was a set of stairs at the side of the building that led up to a door I assumed was for the apartment. There was also a large pergola and hot tub set up on the back roof of the building that was dropped down from the front.

"You live here?"

"Yeah," he shrugged as we made our way up the stairs. "Ace, Knox, and I are silent partners in the bar downstairs. Our friend, Jake, owns the remaining piece and runs the place."

I laughed and shook my head, just another thing I didn't know about Knox. However, it made sense. That was why the guys had been able to move around the place that night without being bothered. Anywhere else there would have been a mob scene. He unlocked the door and held it open for me. When I stepped in I was blown away.

The place was surprisingly clean for a bachelor pad and boasted an amazing open floor plan. You walked directly into the kitchen which was connected to the dining room and living room. No walls separated the rooms, the only way to tell where one ended and the other began was by the contents. Cort closed the door behind us and gestured for me to follow him down a hall on the left. We walked by two bedrooms and a bathroom before he pushed open another door and went in.

I knew it was Knox's room before I crossed the threshold. I could smell him immediately. Cort moved across the room which was colored in greens and browns. The bed was a beautiful log piece. I followed him into the bathroom and he dropped my bag.

"Towels are in the closet over there," he pointed. "Just come out into the kitchen when you're done and we will head out."

"Thank you."

I wasted little time shutting the door behind him and cranking up the water as hot as it could get. The bathroom was large by many standards and boasted not only a jetted tub, but a stand up shower with enough room for more than one person. As soon as the water touched my body I felt all my fears melt away. Knox's smell permeating the air around me put me at ease. I showered quickly. I was antsy to get to my final destination.

Fifteen minutes later, hair still damp, a little make-up on, and my bag repacked, I entered the kitchen. Cort looked up and let out a low whistle. I blushed lightly and shook my head at him. I wore a red henley with the buttons undone, a white cami underneath, dark wash fitted blue jeans, and brown knee-high hiking boots.

"My brother is lucky he met you first," he told me honestly as he led the way back out of the apartment once we had put our jackets on.

I rolled my eyes, but gave him a warm smile. We climbed into the truck and made our journey north. Stopping once for coffee, we reached their parent's house around six o'clock and my nerves were on edge once more. Pulling into the driveway of a beautiful two story farmhouse, I took a deep breath. The house sat back off the main road and was surrounded by white fencing with a red barn out back. The grounds were immaculate and I could picture the vibrant colors of the flowers in the spring even though a light layer of snow covered the ground.

Cort pulled the truck to a stop, turned it off, and jumped out. I froze for a moment and was startled when he opened my door. He gave me a smile and opened the door behind mine to grab my bags while I got out. I took another deep breath and released it. I felt Cort's hand squeeze my shoulder and then his hand found the small of my back to steer me towards the house.

He opened the front door quietly and pushed me in gently ahead of him. The door led directly into the kitchen which was homey, welcoming, and smelled of pancakes and bacon. Cort and Knox's mother was at the stove cooking and their stepfather was setting the table. All movement stopped when we stepped in the door.

"Good morning!" his mother greeted turning from her place at the counter.

"Mom, Dad, this is Mackenzie Shaw," Cort introduced us. "Kenzie, this is my mom, Sharon, and my father, David."

David, from what Knox had told me, was the only father they had ever known. He had been with their mother for twenty years and, at some point, they had just started calling him dad rather than adding the step to it. Their true father had given up all rights, taken off, and never looked back.

I shook both of their hands and glanced around nervously. His mother must have sensed I was uneasy because she shooed Cort off to wake up Knox and settled me at the counter with a fresh cup of coffee while I waited. She asked me about my books and I instantly felt at ease as I told her about my latest release. Minutes later I heard murmured voices coming from the hallway. Sharon turned me towards them and her smile was almost as big as mine.

"Why are you getting me up this early? And why the hell is

mom cooking breakfast already?" I heard Knox ask sleepily and mildly annoyed.

"Your Christmas present is here. You need to see it!" came the reply.

"It couldn't wait until tomorrow?"

Sharon and I giggled, putting our hands over our mouths to muffle the sounds. When they finally rounded the corner, the cowboy I knew was dressed in athletic shorts, a t-shirt, and a backwards fitted baseball cap. He was also rubbing his eyes, so it took him a moment to register that it was me in front of him. I knew the minute he focused because his eyes went wide and his smile was enormous.

I hopped off the stool and met him in the middle of the kitchen. He wrapped me in his arms so tight that I couldn't breathe, but I didn't care. When I felt tears on my cheeks that weren't my own, I knew that I had made the right choice. Pulling away slightly, he brought his hands up to cup my cheeks and kissed me sweetly. I beamed when he was done and wiped away his tears with my hands.

"Merry Christmas, Knox," I whispered.

"Merry Christmas, Mackenzie."

Chapter Ten

*"Admitting one's feelings does not make one weak, admission is
actually a sign of great strength."*

Two months. Well almost two months. That's how
long it had been since I had seen Knox and it was
killing me. Well, maybe not just me. I'm pretty sure
Meghan was seriously rethinking her position as my assistant.
Especially this morning. My mood was less than stellar and it
didn't feel like it was going to get any better. Valentine's Day
looming the following week wasn't helping.

"Why don't you go surprise him again?" Meghan asked
exasperated.

"I can't do that all the time. Plus, I have two signings next
week with the holiday," I told her, which she already knew.

"I know, but girl," she said grabbing my arms and holding
me still in front of her, "you are going to drive us all crazy."

"I'm sorry," I told her sitting down on the couch in my office
with a soft *THUD*. "I've never felt like this before."

"Oh honey," she sympathized coming over and plopping down beside me. "It's called love."

"I know that," I replied. "It's also all the women, a new tour mate, and the distance. FaceTime is almost a tease."

"Might be, but without it you wouldn't have a relationship at all," she pointed out.

I couldn't argue there. Our relationship did hinge on text messages and FaceTime. Prior to Christmas it hadn't bothered me much, but now I couldn't seem to get enough of him. I wanted to hold him, kiss him, and just be with him. I'm not sure what had changed. Maybe it was just my feelings getting stronger, or maybe it was that his mother had told me two things while I was with them for the holiday. The first was that her son had never been comfortable enough to bring any women to the house to meet them, whether it was a surprise or not. The other was that she had never seen him look at anyone the way he had looked at me.

"I'm sorry," I apologized squeezing her hand. "Let's work on preparing for those signings. Valentine's Day is almost as bad as Christmas."

She moaned and rolled over on her stomach to hide her face when I got up. I laughed and grabbed the calendar to see where we were next week. I was so grateful for the women I had in my life. Without them, the distance in my relationship with Knox would have been harder to bear. Leaning over, I kissed her soundly on the cheek and chuckled when she jokingly wiped it off.

The next week was a little easier to deal with since we were so busy getting ready for the signings I was doing and I was attempting to finish my current book. Knox and I talked every night and all was well with us. He was so excited to have Rebecca and her husband on tour with him. I was even able to meet them through FaceTime and she genuinely seemed like a sweet woman. One that was clearly in love with her significant other.

"Are you sure you don't want me to bring him here to meet you?" a sweet lady asked as I signed her book. She was adamant about my being perfect for her grandson and she wanted to run home and bring him back with her.

"I appreciate that you think so highly of me," I told her as I handed the book back to her, "but I'm seeing someone."

"If you change your mind," she said patting my hand and slipping a piece of paper under it, "here is his number."

I nodded and smiled. When she stepped away from the table I handed the paper to Meghan who was laughing behind me. I shushed her and tried not to giggle along with her. When I turned back around to handle the next person in line I found two women my age. One was holding a copy of my latest book along with two of my older ones and the other was engrossed in a Country Chit Chat magazine.

"Do you want them signed to someone specifically?" I asked the woman that held my books like treasures.

"Yes, please," she answered setting them on the table, "to Jennifer."

"I told you something was going on between those two!!!" her friend suddenly squealed. "The chemistry between the two of them on the stage was crazy."

"Who are they writing about now?" I asked with a grin as I signed her friend's books.

"Knox Pride and Rebecca Hall," she informed me. "You should see the two of them on stage singing their new duet. It's simply amazing."

I felt Meghan's hand on my shoulder and I shrugged it off. I knew there wasn't anything going on. I had seen them both with my own two eyes on FaceTime. I had also watched every YouTube video out there looking for exactly that, but all I had seen was two people who are very talented and good at their jobs. I laughed along with the two women as I finished with the books and handed them back to them. When they left I turned to Meghan.

"Can you please go find me that magazine?"

"I'm not sure..."

"Meghan, now please," I cut her off with a little more authority than I normally did.

She scurried off with a confused look on her face and I kept on chugging along through the line of people. Men and women alike were there. I hadn't been kidding when I said that Valentine's Day was a lot like Christmas. Men were looking for those last-minute gifts for their wives and women were looking for that book boyfriend to keep them company.

When I finished up a couple of hours later I got out of my seat and went to where my friend was picking up the extra swag and books that were laid out. She pointed behind her to where our jackets were and I saw not one but four magazines. I looked at her with my eyebrow raised.

"I'm sorry," she apologized continuing to pack.

I put them all in the bag I carried with me that included my purse, water, snacks, and other personal items. I would look at them later when I was in the privacy of my own home. This was exactly what Knox had tried warning me about. Sighing, I helped Meghan finish with clean up. We had one more signing the following day and then I could wallow in my own misery for the holiday. I would be just fine. I trusted him.

By the time the second signing was over I was ready to pull my hair out and hide in a hole. It seemed like everyone was talking about Knox and Rebecca, between magazines and social media. I had ignored my cell phone ever since the prior evening. Knox was trying to get in touch with me, along with my girlfriends, my parents, and my brother. Alicia especially was on a tear. She was convinced she had been right about him. Meghan stood by my side and believed in him, one of the benefits to her knowing him better than the others and her being in touch with Ace.

After I dropped my friend off at her apartment I headed home. It was already dark and the storm they had predicted was starting. I pulled into the garage and sat for a moment before climbing out of my vehicle. My mother had already taken care of the boys so after a quick night check I was back in the house. Making sure all the doors were locked, I lugged my bag up to my bedroom and started the tub. The water was hot enough to practically burn my skin and when it was partially full, I dumped in a cap full of the lilac bath soap I frequently used. The smell immediately filled the room and I took a deep breath to relax myself. When I was satisfied that the tub was full enough I went back to my room, plugged in my phone, and grabbed my robe that was hanging on the corner of the closet door.

Pulling my hair into a messy bun and putting on a headband to catch the stray wispy hairs, I stripped down and put my clothes in the hamper. I was just about to step into the tub when I heard someone pounding on my front door. Hissing, I grabbed my robe and pulled it on, making sure to tighten the belt enough that I didn't show more than I had to to my unwanted guest since it only came to mid-thigh as it was. I didn't know who the heck would be bothering me, but to say I was annoyed was an understatement.

"This had better be good," I muttered as I made my way down the stairs while the pounding continued.

I flicked on the light in the entry way and unlocked the door. When I whipped it open, I was more than surprised to see who was on the other side. Knox stood with his head down and his arms resting on either side of the door frame. Snow dusted his hat and the shoulders of his leather coat, as well as the bag resting on the porch near his feet. When he looked up and his bloodshot eyes met mine I knew why he had come. He stood up and started to speak, but I put my finger over his mouth to silence him. Pulling him inside after he grabbed his bag, I shut and locked the door once again and turned the light off. I then proceeded to lead him upstairs.

I finally turned to him once I had brought him all the way into my bathroom. He looked like hell warmed over. His face was tired and drawn, his eyes red, and his beard scruffy for him. I took his bag from him and set it on the floor.

"Strip," I ordered before I made a lap around the bathroom lighting candles that were set up in various places and finally switching off the light.

When I was done, he was down to his long-sleeved shirt and his jeans. I faced him and untied the belt of my robe. His eyes widened as he took in my nakedness. The look along with the bulge in his pants made me feel powerful. Slowly I let the robe slide down my arms and drop to the floor. Keeping my eyes on him, I stepped into the large claw tub and settled in. There was more than enough room for him to join me, so I waited.

Shaking his head, Knox seemed to come out of his stupor. A slow, sly smile spread across his face as he put his hands behind his head to pull his shirt off. My breath hitched at the play of muscle with the action and my nipples stood at attention despite the hot water. With a twinkle in his eye, he unbuttoned his jeans and shucked both those and his boxer briefs in one motion.

I thought I was going to come just from the magnificent sight of him. Knox was solid everywhere, and I mean everywhere. I felt my body expand to receive him just from looking.

When my eyes met his, the twinkle was gone. They were now filled with a combination of desire and something softer.

He came over to the side of the tub and nudged me forward with his foot as he climbed in behind me. I slid forward so he could get situated. His hands finally came around me to pull my back flush against his chest and I had to suppress a moan when I felt his erection against my backside. I closed my eyes and ran my hands up and down his legs as he used a washcloth to spread body wash from the mini-shelving unit by the tub over my body.

"So, before anything else happens," he stated, "we need to talk about something."

"You're killing the moment, ya know," I teased.

"Oh, I'll get it back," he replied chuckling low and rolling his hips a bit behind me.

"If you want to talk get on with it," I told him as my eyes closed from his movements. "You're losing me, brain wise."

"Talking," he said on a sigh. "About this whole Rebecca thing."

I immediately stiffened in his arms and had to will myself to relax. He had come all the way here. I trusted him. All of the stories and social media posts had to be bothering him as well. Inch by inch my body melted back against him once again.

"I'm sorry. You know nothing has happened, right?" he pleaded.

"Yes, I know that. I have seen the way she and her husband look at each other," I reminded him, especially since Rebecca had stolen Knox's phone during our sessions more than once.

"The same way I look at you," he whispered in my ear, "and for the same reason."

"Oh?" I questioned, shivering from the vibrations of his deep baritone voice.

"I love you Mackenzie Shaw," he confessed, "with everything I am."

My eyes popped open and I spun as much as I could without sending water over the side of the tub. Our eyes locked and I knew that he meant it. He was right. The look he had on his face right now was the same one that had been on Rebecca's husband's face just a few nights ago. It was also on Knox's face in the diner picture. Tears pricked the backs of my eyes.

"I love you too," I replied softly, cupping his face in my hands.

He kissed me gently and I felt his hands move to the back of my head under my hair. I shifted so I had one leg bent under me while the other stretched out behind so that I could get closer to him. Angling my head, I took the angle of the kiss a little deeper and opened my mouth on a moan when he teased my lips with his tongue. I felt a fire deep within me ignite as his hands ran down my neck, across my ribs, and down to cup and squeeze my breasts.

Leaning back without losing eye contact, I pulled the plug to let the water out of the tub. Knox got out and grabbed the closest towel to soak up the excess water on his body. His erection was even harder than before and seemed to strain towards me. I had barely stepped out of the tub myself when Knox's mouth was back on mine and he was drying me off. The feeling of his hands and the towel had me purring and I could feel dampness between my legs despite being towel dried.

A growl came from deep within Knox as he dropped the towel and pulled me tight against him. When I felt his erection against my belly, pulsing, I instantly linked my hands around his neck and jumped up to wrap my legs around his waist. This brought us core to core and I felt his warm hands grip my ass to pull me tighter against him. Panting, he pulled from our kiss to get some air and leaned his forehead against mine. I rolled my pelvis against his and moaned.

"Woman," he groaned, "we aren't going to make it to the bedroom at this rate."

"We don't need to," I gasped as I felt his member moving on its own accord. "Wall, here, now."

"We need protection," he reminded me, squeezing my ass and rocking me back and forth against him.

"I have an IUD," I informed him, reaching down I put one hand between us and teased the top of his penis.

That was all he needed to hear. Moving us the two steps it took to get us to the wall, he shifted away enough to find my entrance and slammed into me. I let out a squeak from the sudden intrusion causing Knox to still in fear. He hadn't hurt me, but his size was definitely not what I was used to. To assure him I was okay, I moved my hips to cause some friction. He pulled out slightly and slid back in slowly multiple times to test my reaction. I closed my eyes and arched my back loving the feeling of him filling me. His mouth found my right nipple and he took it in, rolling it between his teeth and sucking, gently first and then more insistent. The harder suckling had my hands moving to the back of his head to hold him there while my hips worked to increase his pace below.

Shifting slightly to get a better grip on my ass, he slid in and out of me faster and harder. I felt the fire building and knew I was getting closer. He began to moan against my chest as he switched sides and gave the same attention to my other nipple. The vibrations from his mouth and the sounds were enough to send me over the edge and my insides clenched tightly around his member. It was exactly what he needed to follow, seconds later he was straining and ejecting his seed into my body.

It felt like we stood there forever, when it was probably only seconds. My legs were Jell-O around Knox's waist and he gently moved them so I could stand on my own. Grabbing the towel that he had used to dry us moments before, Knox cleaned us up. When he was done, he picked me up and brought me into the bedroom, laying me down on top of the covers. While he returned to the bathroom to blow out the candles, I turned down the bed and pulled my hair out of the messy bun it had been in.

The room soon went dark as all the candles were extinguished in the bathroom. I heard Knox move across the room and the bed dipped when he climbed in behind me. He pulled me against his chest and slid his right arm under my head. His smell and the feel of his chest hair against my back caused my nipples to perk and the warmth to come back between my legs.

I wiggled my butt and instantly felt his erection come back to life. His left hand paused in the circles it was making on my hip and slid forward to the nest between my legs. I arched back into him when his fingers found my clit and started slowly moving back and forth while pinching gently. I pushed my butt into him again as hard as I could and felt his member shift against the pressure. His moan in my ear told me he was just as ready as I was.

"Knox," I panted shifting restlessly, "inside me, now."

My pleading worked. He moved his left hand, but only long enough to guide himself to my opening. His right bent at the elbow bringing my head and upper body closer to his. His left hand came back to push gently at my nest as he slid inside of me. Where the last time had been quick and filled with desire, this time was slow and filled with love. He kept his mouth busy leaving trails up and down my neck and nibbling at my ear. My right hand was intertwined with his while my left helped him to find just the right rhythm with my clit.

Despite the slower pace, my body's reaction to him was just as quick. I held on to him for dear life as my body took over and stars flashed against my closed eyelids. He came at the same time, my walls milking his member for every last drop of his orgasm. This time I cleaned us up using tissues from my bedside table so we didn't have to get up. When I was finished, I snuggled against him and settled my head on his chest. Listening to his heartbeat, steady and strong, under my ear, my eyes started to close.

"I love you, baby," I heard him whisper kissing my hair after and settling his left hand over my right on his chest.

"I love you too," I murmured sleepily, drifting off with a smile on my face and a full heart.

Chapter Eleven

"Being proud of someone can be such a fulfilling feeling, one
that almost makes the accomplishment your own."

Spring came in like lamb, meaning it could only go out like a lion. Other than the fact that I hadn't seen Knox because of his busy tour schedule and my spring signings, things were fairly quiet. I had finished my current book and after my mother had done her editing I had sent it on to my publishing company. Emails had come in here and there from my editor as she worked through it, but for the most part it was peaceful. I wasn't sure if I should be nervous or excited. It had never happened that way.

"So, are we having a pajama party for the ACMs or what?" Meghan asked as she put the last of a new shipment of books on an empty shelf.

"Definitely," I nodded scribbling some brainstorms on a sheet of paper. "Call Alicia and Kelly and invite them too."

"Wahoo! Girls night!" my friend cheered as she pumped her fist in the air.

I pushed back from my desk and turned towards her, laughing. It had been awhile since the four of us had been able to get together. I saw Meghan five days a week most weeks, depending on our schedule, but the others had been crazy busy as well. Kelly had been wedding planning and Alicia had been tied up with her teaching. We had a shopping date for bridesmaid dresses the following week, but this would be more laid back and give us a chance to chat.

"Sorry things have been so nuts around here," I apologized leaning back in my chair.

"Gosh girl, don't apologize," she said sitting down on the floor in front of me, leaning back on her arms and crossing her legs in front of her. "I wish we had known long ago how busy you had been. We could have helped you."

"It started just before I hired you," I told her shaking my head. "There really hadn't been much else to do. I would write a few days a week and I would schedule and organize on the others."

"Do you even have an inkling of how awesome you are?" Meghan asked. "You juggle stuff here at home, friends, family, your writing, and now things with Knox. Just. Simply. Amazing."

I blushed and got up to stretch. I really wasn't that great. Sure, my books had started to take off in the past year but that had been after my mother had introduced me to one of her publisher friends. The signings seemed to help as well, however, that was all me. I enjoyed hearing what my readers thought and meeting them one-on-one. As for my stuff at home, the horses kept me sane. The riding and the few riding lessons I taught during the spring/summer/fall helped me to relax and get out of my head for a little while. Knox, well, he had been totally unplanned and the best thing that had happened to me in some time.

"I don't know about amazing," I said to her shrugging, "but I am definitely a happy girl."

We finalized plans for the following night and decided we would have Chinese take-out and ice cream sundaes for dessert. The show was scheduled to start at seven so we figured six for dinner. We were all excited and even planned on a sleepover though Kelly and Alicia would have to leave early for work the next morning. It was a perfect ladies' night in.

That night Knox was ecstatic to hear that I would have them all with me for company. He was nervous since he was nominated for three awards, Video of the Year, Male Vocalist of the Year, and Song of the Year. It broke my heart not to be there with him, but we had agreed that this soon in our relationship was too early to come out in public. It was all still so new. Our conversation didn't last long because he had pre-parties to attend, yet he let me know that he would have his phone during the show so I could reach him if I needed to. I was pretty sure that was his way of letting me know he would be texting me because he was nervous.

Getting the boys settled in around five o'clock the next night, I was back in the house and in my pajamas by 5:30 when Meghan showed up with her bag in tow. By the time she had changed and we had poured two glasses of wine, the other two were pulling in the driveway. The delivery guy was directly behind them and I'm certain we scared him with all of our squealing. The timing couldn't have been more perfect.

"What time does red carpet start?" Alicia asked dropping her bag by the doorway when she reentered the living room.

"I think it starts....now," Kelly screeched reaching for the remote.

"We aren't going to miss much ladies," I told them as I organized the take-out containers on the coffee table.

"How can you be so calm?!" Meghan asked as she put paper plates down along with plastic silverware.

"My heart is pounding and I feel sick," I informed her draining my wine glass. "The cool outside is just for show."

The girls laughed as the red carpet filled the TV screen. We each grabbed a plate and started piling up food while the announcers talked to some of the actors, actresses, and singers that walked by. I wasn't completely sure that we would see Knox so I scooted to the kitchen to grab the bottle of wine that Meghan and I had already opened. Suddenly I heard screaming coming from the living room. Bottle in hand, I entered to find Alicia turning up the volume and none other than my man filling the screen. His black jeans hugged his legs firmly and his black blazer covered a hunter green button-up dress shirt. His head was bare of his hat leaving his hair wavy and me itching to run my fingers through it as always.

"Knox Pride! Congratulations on your nominations tonight!" said the gorgeous blonde with the microphone.

"Thank you very much," he replied with a large smile.

"How is it that such a handsome man like you is always at these events without a beautiful woman on your arm?"

"Well, she was kind of busy tonight," he answered chuckling and his cheeks took on a pinkish hue. "Maybe for the next one."

With that comment he ducked away and into the throngs of people behind him. My mouth dropped open and the girls had all turned to gawk at me. We had talked briefly about my attending the CMT Awards with him in June, but we hadn't made any solid plans. Nor had we discussed leaking our relationship to the public.

"What was that?" Kelly asked with a smile.

"Damned if I know," I said honestly.

"After that," Meghan stated, "he is being tweeted like crazy! Look at this!"

Sure enough his name was climbing the ranks in popularity on Twitter. Most of it was about whether or not he had a mystery girlfriend while a few were woman claiming to be said woman. We laughed over those. As we were calming down and starting to eat, my phone went off. Alicia tossed it to me after looking at the screen to see who it was. Knox. I raised my eyebrow at her, he must finally be growing on her.

So sorry! Hate being put on the spot like that. I can't lie! <3 u!

Chuckling, I read it to the girls. I got laughs and awwws. Rolling my eyes, I replied and went back to my plate. I knew if I didn't eat supper now I would never be able to when the show started and awards were being handed out. We all finished eating and cleaned up just in time for the actual show to start. I had already heard from my mother and Matt was texting Kelly. I guess he and Brandon were at their house watching. Everyone was so excited for Knox. I couldn't have been happier.

"Here we go!!!" Meghan hollered as Kelly and I gathered ice cream sundae stuff in the kitchen.

The show had been on for half an hour and we had been fidgeting with excitement to see the awards Knox was nominated for and for he and Rebecca to perform. When we entered the room, Alicia was turning up the TV once again and I could hear the beginning strings of "Without You". We quickly put everything down on the table and the four of us huddled on the couch to watch. Their chemistry on stage was impeccable. The song was a perfect fit for their voices and my heart swelled just listening to them.

"Wow! Goosebumps!" Alicia whispered when they were done and the show had moved to a commercial.

"Yeah," Meghan seconded.

"You must be so proud of him," Kelly said looking over at me with a huge smile.

"I am," I told them as we shuffled around to make our sundaes. "He is so good at what he does."

Directly after the commercial the first award he was nominated for came up. It was Video of the Year. We were all on the edge of our seats as they went through the artists. Even though we were in my living room, we cheered and screamed when they called Knox's name. Unfortunately, it went to someone else. I laughed as Meghan mumbled that it should have been his and how his video was ten times better than the one that took home the award. I adored my friends for all of their support.

Another performer came out as we moaned in anticipation. We just wanted to know if Knox had won either of the other two. Finishing our sundaes, we screeched when they announced the artists up for Song of the Year. You could have heard a pin drop though when they drew out reading off the name.

"And Song of the Year goes to.....Just Ask, written by Knox and Cort Pride!!"

The four of us bounded off the couch screaming and hugging each other. Within seconds all hell had broken loose. Our cell phones all started going off and bowls were falling off the coffee table. We quieted long enough to hear his speech and when he was done there wasn't a dry eye in the house. While the show went to a commercial, we quickly cleaned up our mess and returned text messages. I sent an extra one to Knox with a bunch of hearts and an all caps *I LOVE YOU!!!*.

A few more performances and one award later, it was time for Male Vocalist of the Year. The men nominated along with Knox were great performers. I may have been partial to my man, but I didn't know how they ever made these decisions. It was so hard! We all stood to hear the announcement and I thought I was going to throw up from the eagerness.

"Your Male Vocalist of the Year is," the actress sang out as she struggled with the envelope. *"Knox Pride!!!"*

The screams were deafening. We jumped around grabbing for each other as Knox made his way to the stage. When he reached the microphone we quieted, tears streaming down all of our faces. I was so happy for him. Again, he thanked his family, producers, band and of course the fans. Just before he finished he looked down at the award and paused.

"One last thank you," he said with a strangled voice. *"To that special someone watching from home, I love you and this is that much more exciting because of you."*

I sat down with a *THUMP* and cried like a baby. The girls gathered around me, holding me and handing me tissues. I was so overwhelmed with the feelings I had for this man. He was everything I had dreamed of and more, and he had just acknowledged my importance to him on national TV. The whole thing was surreal.

"Here!" Alicia exclaimed putting my vibrating cell phone into my hands.

"Knox?!"

"Hey baby! Did you see?!" his voice held tears, but I could tell his smile ran ear-to-ear.

"I did! I am so excited for you!"

"Did you hear my speech?" he asked, a little quieter.

"I did. I love you too and I can't wait to be by your side at the next awards show."

I heard him let out a shaky breath and compose himself. I ached to be there with him to celebrate the honors he had just received. I could only hope that the next time our schedules would allow me to be. I would have to go over things with Meghan in the next few days.

"I have to go, baby. I'll call you when I can. I love you."

With that he was gone. The girls and I finished watching

the show, still fidgeting with the excitement of Knox's awards. Meghan got a kick out of checking all his social media sites. People were still speculating about who his "special someone" could be, while a few women were still claiming to be her. "They wish," she would mutter as she continued to click around.

A couple hours later as I settled into bed my phone signaled a FaceTime session from Knox. I was confused. I figured he would be attending after parties and that I wouldn't hear from him until the next day. Without bothering to turn on a light or check my hair, I swiped my finger across the screen.

"Hey handsome," I greeted snuggling into my pillow. "This is a nice surprise."

"Hi beautiful," he returned. "Just needed to see your face."

"Everything okay? I figured you would be out partying."

"On my way, actually," he said undoing the top two buttons of his shirt and running his hand through his hair. "You *are* coming to the next one."

"That bad?" I asked chuckling.

"Have you seen social media?!"

"Yep, Meghan was keeping tabs."

"She would be," he laughed, seeming to relax a bit. "Some are saying that I was talking about Rebecca in my speech and just said it was someone at home to hide our affair."

"Knox, I know the truth," I reminded him. "Enjoy the night with your friends and celebrate those amazing awards."

"I will," he promised letting out a breath as the car seemed to pull to a stop. "Next one? Promise?"

"I promise! Scout's honor."

"Okay," he relented. "I love you baby girl."

"I love you too and I'm so proud of you. You deserved those awards more than you know."

Blowing me a kiss, he ended the session. I plugged my phone in and got comfortable. The next awards show was two months away. Guess it was time to get used to being in the public eye because my quiet life was about to become nonexistent.

Chapter Twelve

"Putting yourself out there for the world to see opens up every piece of your life, it exposes you to be ridiculed and judged."

"Ma'am, we're here," the driver informed me as we pulled in front of a rather large and beautiful hotel, never mind high-end looking.

"I told you, call me Mackenzie."

"Sorry, ma'am...I mean Mackenzie," he apologized putting the car in park.

I shook my head as he got out and came around to let me out. While it was nice to have someone else navigate traffic in an unfamiliar town, I wasn't sure I would ever get used to being carted around. When my door opened, I stepped out into the summer Nashville air. We weren't far from Cash's. I wasn't sure why we were staying here and not at his apartment, but I shrugged and followed Ted to the rear of the car to grab my bags.

"I can take them," I told him shouldering my smaller bag

and pulling the handle up on the other to wheel it away from the curb.

"Are you sure?"

"Yes, despite what Ace and Knox told you. I'm fully capable."

"That's exactly what they told me," he said chuckling. "Lexie will meet you inside, I already let her know that you were here."

I nodded and waved to him as he moved back around the car to get in and leave. I took a deep breath and started towards the front door. Both Ace and Knox had been tied up, so I had told them I would be fine getting to the hotel. Instead they had sent a driver to pick me up and they had hired someone to help with my hair and make-up. I entered through the doors currently being held by two bell boys and instantly was met by a spunky young redhead I assumed to be Lexie since she carried a sign with my name on it. Before I could utter a word, she was dragging me towards the elevators and chatting about the awards show that night.

We went up ten floors before we came to a stop and when we stepped out a couple of security guards met us. She flashed them a badge and we continued down the hall. A few doors down she slid a card and let us in. Entering, I was speechless. It wasn't just a room, but an enormous suite. Knox had gone above and beyond. His bag sat in the living room and I could faintly smell his cologne which helped me to relax.

"Okay, let's get you cleaned up and then we can get started on your hair and make-up," Lexie commanded as she led me into the bedroom. "You can leave your bags here. Go ahead and take a shower, when you're done just put on the robe."

Taking her lead, I put my bags near the bureau. I grabbed my toiletry bag and the robe dangling from her fingers before heading into the bathroom. Once I was alone I turned the water on as hot as I could bear it and stripped down. I knew we had semi-limited time, especially since my plane had been late, but I wanted to soak up my alone time while I could and unwind. My nerves were a bit frayed with the traveling and the idea of having so many sets of eyes on me.

I gave myself a couple of minutes of just letting the water roll down my body before I got to business. When I was done, I dried off and wrapped up in the robe. Brushing my teeth, I gave myself a pep talk and some encouragement. *Tonight will be amazing and unforgettable. I am strong and beautiful.* A knock at the door jumped me and interrupted my thoughts. Taking a shaking breath, I wiped my mouth and stepped out.

"Gosh, you're beautiful," Lexie commented as I sat down in the chair she had pulled up beside the French doors over-looking the courtyard. "This will be easy."

"What are you thinking?" I asked her. I wasn't even sure what I would be wearing.

"Waves and a little pulled up. Simple, yet elegant."

"Do you know what I'm wearing?"

"Rebecca didn't show you?" she questioned as she started separating my hair to blow dry it.

"Nope," I said. "Knox told me he had left it in her capable hands."

"It's perfect for you," she replied. "Just relax and enjoy the pampering."

I wasn't going to argue with that. Closing my eyes, I sat and felt the tension drain from my muscles while she ran her fingers through my hair expertly drying it. Moments later I jumped and my eyes popped open as someone touched my foot. I found a young brunette smiling at me with a small table sitting beside her. When I saw what her intent was, I happily gave her back my foot and closed my eyes again. Eventually I heard the blow dryer turn off and Lexie shifted to using product and a curling iron.

"So, I'm nosey," she stated. "How did you meet Knox?"

"Right here in Nashville at a bar," I told both ladies, opening my eyes with a smile.

Knox and I had known people would ask. We had decided it was easier to tell them all the truth, only leaving out a few things like the fact that he and Cort had ownership in said bar. From there they asked how long we had officially been a couple and what I did for a living. They were sweet and were great practice for the millions of times I would have to tell the story later. Time passed quickly and before I knew it, Casey, the brunette, and Lexie were done. My nails were done in a beautiful tie dye pattern, fingers and toes, but neither of them would let me see a mirror yet. I could feel the waves on my shoulders, however, beyond that I was clueless.

"Your shoes and outfit are in the closet," Lexie let me know as she finished packing up her stuff and headed for the door. "Wait to look until you have the whole package put together."

I hugged them both and thanked them profusely. The bedroom door clicked behind them. I moved to the closet once I was alone and pulled open the door. I was stunned by what I found. Hanging was a gorgeous pant suit in similar colors to those that adorned my nails, a pearl white with purples, greens, and blues. All in pale colors. There were slits in each leg that I guessed would come up to my thigh and deep v's front and back with crisscrossing straps. It would be form fitting and leave little to the imagination. Thank goodness I hadn't planned on wearing a bra. The shoes were strappy and had a 3-inch heel.

Untying the robe, I took it off and placed it on the bed. I grabbed a slip of a thong that was in my toiletry bag and put it on before reaching for the suit. It fit my body like a glove and felt good against my skin. I strapped on the shoes and when I stood back up I sucked in a breath. Turning to the full-length mirror on the opposite wall I almost fell over. I looked amazing, sexy, confident, and every part the famous country singer's girl-friend. Lexie had created large waves in my hair just as she had said and pulled a little up with bobby pins on each side to keep it out of my face. My make-up was simple and you could barely tell I was wearing any except for my eyes, they seemed to "pop" out of my face.

"Wow," I muttered moving slightly to get the whole effect.

"My thoughts exactly," Knox voiced from the doorway.

I hadn't even heard him open the door. When I faced him completely I couldn't form any words. He wore the same outfit he wore to every awards show, dark jeans, a button up dress shirt, boots, and a blazer. Tonight the button up was the same pearl white as my suit. His beard was trimmed and the waves in his hair had me clasping my hands together to keep me from touching them. Brown eyes sparkled and his smile was bigger than I had ever seen.

"You look pretty amazing yourself," I complimented moving towards him.

"Oh, do I?" he teased taking the last steps to bring us toe-to-toe.

"You know, I haven't put lipstick on yet."

I had barely finished speaking when his mouth came crashing down on mine, one of his hands cupped my neck while the other was on the small of my back holding me close to him. Our tongues stroked each other and when I felt his erec-tion against my belly I groaned into his mouth. The sound must have cleared his head a bit because the kisses became gentle before ceasing all together. We both panted lightly as we caught our breaths, foreheads touching.

"You have very little, if anything, underneath your clothes," he whispered accusingly.

"Very little," I replied chuckling and turning away to touch up my make-up and put on lipstick.

"It's going to be a long night," I heard him mumble as he adjusted himself and headed towards the living room.

I laughed as I put a few things into my tiny matching clutch. I placed the band around my wrist and with a final look in the mirror I made my way through the suite to where Knox was waiting. He was looking out a set of French doors in the living room and again I was taken back by how handsome he was. My heart went *pitter pat* with the sight of him. I couldn't wait to tell the whole world he belonged to me.

"You ready?" he asked turning towards me.

"As ready as I'll ever be," I told him reaching for his hand.

We made our way out of the suite and into the hallway. Rebecca and her husband, Mark, were coming towards us and I felt myself relax even more. A couple of familiar faces were better than none. She raved about the suit and how good it looked and I thanked her graciously for picking it out as the four of us headed to the elevator. Knox squeezed my hand while we rode down. He knew I was nervous.

When we reached the lobby I was surprised to find it empty. The quiet didn't last long though. Crowds lined the walkway to our limo. Knox released my hand to put it on the small of my back to steer me quickly and efficiently behind the other couple and to our ride. We all climbed in and moments later were on the short drive to the center where the CMAs were held.

Rebecca chatted the whole way and before I knew it, the limo was pulling to a stop. I gripped Knox's hand like a life line and was relieved when he waved at the other couple to exit the car first. The driver opened the door and they stepped out. He closed it behind them, but I knew he would be opening it again soon.

"You okay?" he asked squeezing my hand with one hand and cupping my cheek with the other.

"Yep, just a little nervous," I admitted. "There are a lot of people out there and a lot of people watching."

"You look beautiful," he told me placing a gentle kiss on the tip of my nose. "All we have to do is smile pretty for a little while and then we will be in the building. They will love you."

"You should be the one anxious about tonight," I giggled placing my free hand on my chest. "I'm sorry. I'll be fine."

The door opened again and he gave me a reassuring smile. Knox got out first and when he reached back for my hand to help me, I drummed up a smile and placed a foot on the ground. Climbing out and bringing myself to my full height I saw the red carpet ahead of us. Rebecca and Mark weren't far off, chatting with someone with a microphone. Knox took my hand in his and we slowly made our way forward. We didn't get far before we were summonsed for pictures.

I was amazed that no one questioned us about who I was. I saw the looks we were getting out of the corner of my eye. Some were curious, while others were daggers aimed at me for being on his arm. We were almost half way down when we were stopped for another picture. This time Knox turned to look at me. His eyes were warm and his smile soft. I got lost in the connection and when his lips met mine in a sweet kiss I let myself forget everything else. His right hand rested gently on my lower back and his left came up to cover the one that I had on his chest. Parting, he smiled again and turned back towards the person taking the picture. That's when it happened.

"Knox, who is that beautiful woman with you?"

"How long has this been going on?"

"What about Rebecca?"

My head started to spin from all the questions. Knox still looked cool as a cucumber, but I saw him searching the crowd. I could tell when he found who he was looking for because he smiled and tugged on my hand. He led me down the carpet a bit to a blonde woman talking with another singer and her husband. The crowd behind us buzzed, yet Knox seemed adamant that this was the person he wanted to talk to. When she finished, she turned to us with a toothy smile. It was the same woman that had interviewed him during the ACM Awards.

"Knox Pride! It's so good to see you and sporting a beautiful woman on your arm no less," she greeted reaching out to bring us closer to her.

"Good to see you too, Dianne," he returned, putting his arm around my waist once again as we settled in front of her. "I wanted to introduce you to my girlfriend, romance novelist, Mackenzie Shaw."

"Oh my gosh! I have read all of your books!" she gushed. "You guys are the perfect couple and you look so happy together."

"We are very happy," Knox told her as he looked me in the eye. "I was lucky enough to run into her at a bar here in Nashville eight months ago and she stole my heart from the moment I set eyes on her."

"Awwww," she crooned. "That is so sweet. It must make tonight that much more special."

"It does," he agreed.

The two continued to talk about the awards he was nominated for tonight, Male Video of the Year and Breakthrough Video of the Year. They also discussed his wins at the ACMs and when they were done turned to me about my latest book. I gave her a quick rundown and let her and the rest of the world know it was set to release in just a couple weeks. She wrapped up with us and congratulated us again on our relationship and our separate endeavors. Stepping away, Knox steered me towards the building where Rebecca and Mark were waiting by the door.

"You are awfully fussy about who you talk to," I teased earning a true relaxed smile from Knox.

"I want to make sure our story gets out and gets out correctly," he told me. "As it is there will be some outrageous stuff put out there that we can't control."

"I'm not worried about it," I let him know just as we were reaching our friends. "The whole world knows you're mine now."

He laughed and kissed me soundly before directing me forward. We chatted with the other couple as we made our way in to our seats. Rebecca was friendly and warm. She filled me in on who was crushing on Knox and who would be welcoming of me. Normally I wasn't a gossip type girl, but as we moved around people to get to where we would be sitting I got dirty looks from those she said I would and smiles with nods from those she said would be accepting. I kept my face light and my lips turned up. I didn't want anyone to have a reason to trash talk Knox if I could help it.

We found our seats and I was disappointed that we weren't near our friends, however we were seated next to some veterans of the country music world that were more than happy to see us. They were fully supportive of Knox and his climb up the ladder in the industry. They were also curious about us as a couple and in what I did. When the wives found out I was a writer they both immediately put my name in their phones and promised to read one of my books as soon as they could.

By the time the show started I was relaxed and comfortable. I crossed my legs and slid my left hand onto Knox's thigh. He shifted with a grin and leaned over to put his arm across my lap and place his hand on my leg where the slit rode up. I placed my free hand on his to keep him from moving and heard a low chuckle from beside me. I grinned in return.

The show started very quickly. Before I knew it Knox was slipping out of his seat and headed to the back of the stage to prep for his performance with Rebecca. I was so excited to see them in person that I was dancing around in my seat a bit. An actor came out to announce their song and I cheered along with the crowd. Knox started the song and sang in his deep baritone voice for three verses before she came out to pick up the chorus with him. While she sang her verses, he looked to the crowd and flashed a smile that had his dimple showing. When they were done, I screamed and whistled.

"That's awesome," one of the women beside me said placing her hand on my arm.

"What's that?"

"That you know he loves you and that the chemistry up on that stage is just between performers."

I smiled at her and squeezed her hand before turning back to the stage. One of Knox's awards was up immediately so unfortunately he wouldn't make it back to his seat before it was called. Breakthrough Video of the Year was announced along with the nominees. I gripped my hands together so tight that they hurt while we waited for the actress and actor to say who the winner was. When they finally did, it wasn't him. I was bummed, yet I knew he was looking forward to the other award more.

He finally made his way back while a couple of other performers took the stage and another award was handed out. Sliding in beside me, he again reached across my lap with his arm and put his hand directly on my bare skin. I saw him smile out of the corner of my eye and I just shook my head as I laced my fingers through his.

A few songs later Rebecca and an actor came out to announce the award for Male Video of the Year. I gripped Knox's hand as they read off the nominees. He remained calm beside me, but his hand was holding mine just as tight. When they read off the winner I was hauled to my feet and gripped against a solid body. He had done it again! My eyes filled with tears as he pulled away enough to kiss me before he headed towards the stage with another gentleman I assumed was the director.

I was so proud of him. I listened while the director said his thanks and while Knox did his for his fans, band, family and eventually me. I was surprised. I hadn't done anything to get him to this point, he had done it all himself. I was just lucky enough to be along for the ride. His career was starting to take off just as our relationship was. I only hoped that they could both hold on strong.

Chapter Thirteen

"Writing a book gives people a story to enjoy,
writing a book gives people a piece of your soul."

"Oh.My.God!" I heard a voice exclaim from behind me. "It is you!"

I turned around and looked at where the voice came from. I had been reading the label on a gallon of juice when she had spoken. It was an older lady who was alone, but her comment had drawn the attention of two others in the aisle near her. I pointed to myself in question because she didn't look at all familiar. She nodded and rushed over, pulling her cart in behind me so that she didn't block anyone.

"Do I know you?" I asked confused.

"Probably not, but I certainly know who you are," she gushed pulling out her phone and showing me a picture of Knox and myself from the prior week.

"Oh," I stammered unsure how to react.

"Could you please sign this?" she pleaded handing me her grocery list. "Gosh, I wish I had your book with me."

Her last comment warmed me. She not only recognized me for being with Knox, but she knew who I was as an author. I signed her list and once I handed it back to her I commenced to rummaging around in my purse. I found my own phone and opened up a note pad on it.

"How about this," I said, "I'll mail you a signed copy of my new book when it comes out?"

"Really?!" she asked dancing in place.

"You just made my day," I told her putting my hand on her arm. "Of course."

The woman thanked me more times than I could count. Once she was on her way I turned back to my juice. I had barely placed it in my cart when two more women approached me. That was how it continued to go. It took me 45 minutes to purchase five items. I kept getting stopped for autographs and even a couple pictures. It was great publicity for my release party at the local library, yet by the time I finally made it out to my car I was kind of frazzled.

Life became a whirlwind after that. I knew that when my relationship with Knox came out that things would change and that there would be some people who wouldn't like it, however I hadn't realized how much things would alter. There were no more quick trips anywhere and I suddenly had friends coming out of the woodwork. The good news was that they had all respected my privacy as far as my house went. My 10 acres abutted my brother's 10 acres as well as my parents' 50 and I was the last house on our dead-end road. No one had shown up or followed me there.

Meghan had also proved to me during this time that she was the perfect choice for my assistant. While I was preparing for the release of one book and starting another, she was madly keeping up with social media, mail, and phone calls. All that traffic had at least doubled and my friend hadn't missed a beat.

She had even enlisted Alicia and Kelly to help on a few week-nights. I couldn't have been happier to be doing what I loved and to be surrounded by my friends.

"UPS?" Alicia asked looking out the window of my office one afternoon when we heard a noise.

"Books!" Meghan and I screeched at the same time.

We had been waiting for the order to come in and had started getting nervous considering the release party was that weekend. Racing down the stairs, we ran into each other at the front door in a fit of giggles. The other two weren't far behind us. Flinging the door open, we met the UPS man just emerging from his truck with a dolly and three large boxes.

Squealing, we danced in place as we waited for him to get to us. When he dropped the boxes, he chuckled at us and used his box opener to slice the top of one of them. Nick had been my delivery man since I had started writing and was also a good friend of Matt's, so he was used to the excitement that came with a box of new books. Waving to him as he headed back to his truck Meghan and I flipped open the box and dug past packing paper to get to the actual books.

Alicia and Kelly joined us just as I pulled one out. Tears instantly filled my eyes. The cover was even more amazing in person than it was on the computer. My name and the title *The Woman I Want To Be* were encrusted in gold against a picture of a lake and trees at sunset. Barely visible at the bottom of the picture was a dock with the shadows of two people dangling their feet in the water.

"Oh Kenzie," Kelly gasped. "It's gorgeous."

"It's perfect," I stated pulling my phone out of my pocket to snap a picture and send it to Knox.

Matt showed up to pick up Kelly just in time to help us get the boxes into the living room. Meghan and I would do a physical count at some point this week and figure out what needed to come with us to the release party. My brother pulled out a book as he set the last box down and a smile spread across his face. I knew he had never read any of my books, but he was proud as a peacock at what I had accomplished.

"They look awesome, Ken," he voiced coming over and giving me a hug.

"Thanks," I replied gripping him tightly in return.

Alicia and Meghan left right behind Kelly and Matt so I made my way out to bring the boys up from their daytime pasture and give them their supper. I was just finishing up when I felt my phone vibrate against my hip. On my way back to the house I checked it and found a message from Knox.

So proud of you, baby! It looks amazing!! <3 Wish I could be there this weekend. Love you!

Unfortunately, with him being on tour and grabbing studio time in between he wouldn't be able to make it back for the release party. We had planned it as a BBQ theme on Saturday night figuring it would draw a larger crowd. Half the proceeds would benefit the local library, and Knox and his crew had signed 100 CDs for us to sell as well. I was bummed he couldn't be there, but I knew this was the type of situation we would have to get used to with our relationship.

Days later I was packing up my vehicle for the release party when I heard the crunching of tires. I knew it wasn't Meghan because she was meeting me there. She, Matt, and Kelly were setting up and getting the grill going while I was bringing my books. I was surprised when I looked up and found Alicia headed towards me. Our friendship had been tense lately. She still wanted to think the worst of Knox and I couldn't understand why.

"Hey," I greeted shutting the back door of my vehicle. "I thought you were going to meet us all down there?"

"I was going to" she started, staring at the ground and shuffling her feet in the dirt, "but I wanted to apologize first."

"Apologize?" I asked turning to face her.

"Yeah, I haven't exactly been on Knox's side or supportive of you and your happiness lately."

"True," I laughed lightly.

"It broke my heart to see how down you were when things went south with you and Brandon. I just hate the idea of you going through that again. I want you to be happy like Kelly and I are."

"I appreciate that you love me that much," I told her reaching out to grip her hands with mine. "However, I wasn't really that upset when things ended between us. I was more upset that I had ever let myself get into that position. Knox is different and I hope that you can see that someday."

"I have and I'm so sorry," she said smiling through her tears.

I hugged her for all I was worth. I hated the idea of a man causing a rift between us since we had been friends for so long, but Knox was not someone I was easily going to give up. She helped me put a few more things in my car and we headed out. She rode with me and I figured if she wanted to come back before me, she could just take my car and I would hitch a ride with someone else.

Pulling into the library parking lot I was shocked at how many people were already there. My family, friends, and even Brandon and his girlfriend Emmy, were all busy setting things up. Alicia and I pulled around the back and started to unload boxes. It wasn't long before Brandon and Matt joined us to help bring things upstairs and into the main part of the library. They disappeared when we no longer needed the manpower and we commenced setting up the new books as well as some of my older ones.

Twenty minutes later, we were back downstairs mingling

and eating burgers and fruit salad with a bunch of people. There had to be at least 75 people there eating and chatting. Others were slowly trickling in and going directly into the library. The plan was to feed everyone first and then to do a short reading along with autographs and pictures. I recognized most of the people there, but did notice that we had some there that definitely weren't there for the books. They were there to scope me out.

"You ready to head in?" Meghan asked handing me a water and taking my now empty plate.

"Yep," I nodded. "Let's get started."

I went into the building and met up with Mrs. Crane, the head librarian. She had been there since I was a teenager and was very excited for the opportunity. We decided that I would read an excerpt from *The Woman I Want To Be* and after I would sign books for anyone that wanted one. The board of directors for the library would then provide everyone with strawberry shortcake for dessert.

I settled in at the front of the room and skimmed the book I had already marked a few passages in. It was a mixed crowd of men, women, and children so I wanted to pick something that would appeal to everyone. I found one that was about the main character of the book realizing what she wanted from her life and what her true passion was. It fit perfectly with the title. When I looked up I was surprised to see the large reading room bursting at the seams.

I looked around and greeted everyone with a smile. I noticed a woman looking at me intently and I nodded in her direction. Her face was hard and didn't even crack with a smile when I acknowledged her. Turning to Mrs. Crane, who was about to introduce me, I shook it off. I had known some people would show up to check out "Knox Pride's girlfriend", not "Mackenzie Shaw, Author".

I read my passage and let myself get lost in it. When I finished, the crowd clapped. Questions immediately started and ranged from my writing process to the next book I was working on. I was happy that they weren't focused on Knox and our relationship, but on my books and what I did. For a half hour Meghan and I fielded everything the group threw at us. People had been curious about what I did when I wasn't writing and what part my assistant played in the whole thing. The adrenaline was flowing and I couldn't hold back the smile that was on my face. That was until the woman I had noticed a while ago spoke up.

"I have a question," she stated putting up her hand.

"Sure," I welcomed her to the front of the crowd where I could see her better.

"How do you feel knowing that you have taken Knox Pride from another woman?"

Everyone in the room grew silent. My parents looked at me, and Alicia and Kelly moved so that they flanked Meghan and I. I took a deep breath and looked closely at her. I still didn't recognize her, however she did have a bit of a southern drawl to her voice. Meghan put her hand on my arm to signal that I didn't need to say anything. I shook my head at her and turned back to the woman who now had her arms crossed and was tapping her foot.

"It was my understanding that Knox was single when we met. I never would have gotten involved with him if I had known otherwise."

"You bitch!" she shrieked moving to step towards me.

"Angela! Enough!" I heard a familiar voice shout from the doorway.

People moved and Knox came to the front of the room. I could see flashes from people's camera phones and I knew this would be all over social media in a matter of seconds. His eyes met mine and were filled with anger, love, and sympathy. Cort followed him and smiled at me from behind his brother. They stopped in front of us and I could see Alicia's face out of the corner of my eye. She wanted to wring his neck, but I don't think she realized this was beyond his control.

"Hey baby," he said hugging me and kissing my forehead. "This was not how I wanted to surprise you."

"No worries," I told him stepping back. "It probably won't be the last."

"I hate to interrupt your lovely reunion," Angela chimed in, "but everyone needs to know that this woman is a homewrecker and only wants to use Knox for his fame."

"Angela, we were done long before I met Mackenzie," Knox muttered moving closer to her to keep most of the room from hearing what was going on. "You are very well aware of that and you are the one who wanted me for my fame. This woman doesn't need me to get her name out there, she has done that all on her own."

My heart fluttered at the comment. My parents smiled at me from behind Knox's ex-girlfriend. They hadn't met him officially, yet I could tell that they loved him for that alone. Meghan moved closer to me and gripped my hand with hers. I gave her a reassuring smile and squeezed it.

"I can't believe you!" Angela exclaimed and before anyone could stop her I heard a resounding slap as her hand connected with Knox's face, just above his beard.

I moved to step between them only to be stopped by my girlfriends and Cort who had grabbed her arm and was escorting her out. A few other women followed them out, but for the most part the crowd cheered. Knox turned back towards me with an embarrassed smile and rubbed the back of his neck. I put my hand on his face and brought it up so our eyes connected. Kissing him quickly on the lips we moved back to where I had been set up to sign books.

"I apologize everyone," Knox addressed the room. "Please grab your books and get up here to have my girl sign them. Also, don't forget half the proceeds today go to the library and that there is strawberry shortcake for everyone to enjoy."

With that, the drama was forgotten and people lined up. I gave Knox a grateful smile and started chatting with the first woman to approach me. For the first time that I could remember I didn't have mothers or grandmothers pushing numbers at me. Instead, they would quietly congratulate me on my relationship with Knox and ask if they could have a picture with him. He and Cort stood off to my right handing out the autographed CDs they had brought. We even had some that requested pictures of the two of us.

All in all, it was a productive evening. The library was so happy with the turnout and the donations that they invited us back when my next book came out. We readily agreed and started packing up what inventory remained. Meghan and Cort took the first batch of books out, leaving Knox and me alone.

"That was not how I pictured tonight going," he informed me as he picked up a box and put it on the table we had spread the books out on.

"Despite your friend flying all the way here to put on a show, it was a good night," I said laughing.

"I'm really sorry about her," Knox told me turning me to face him with his hands on my hips.

"It wasn't exactly something you could have predicted."

"I should have known something was up with her though. Since the CMAs she has been texting me and calling me. I reiterated it was over and started ignoring her. I never thought she would take it this far."

"No one got hurt, minus your face," I reminded him

cupping his face in my hands. "Everyone had fun and we made some money for the library. Plus, I get to cuddle with you for a few hours before you have to ship out. Again, I say that all in all it was a pretty good night."

"Have I told you how lucky I am to have such an amazing woman like you in my life?" he asked brushing his lips across mine.

"Not lately," I sighed with a grin, "but please feel free to remind me."

Chapter Fourteen

"Watching the most important person in your life do what they love is an amazing feeling, it's contagious."

Flying was becoming my thing, I decided. Since I had started dating Knox I had put more frequent flyer miles on than I ever had. However, it didn't change the fact that I hated it. Stepping off the plane my legs were Jell-O and my stomach was rolling. Next time I was going to stick with a larger airport and a bigger plane.

It was the middle of July and Knox was playing at Jamboree In The Hills. I had decided to fly out and spend the whole four days with him. The event was a festival of country music out in the middle of an enormous hay field in Morristown, Ohio. I had been years ago with my family, but this time I would be backstage with Knox and all the others. Fifteen singers/bands would play throughout the event. It was going to be a blast and I was looking forward to the time off!

The heat and humidity slapped me in the face as I made my way across the tarmac to the airport and I was grateful I had decided on a light-weight cotton dress to travel in. My stomach protested the weather along with the flight so I was relieved when I saw Ace immediately upon entering the building. I had shoved all the clothes I needed into my carry-on for my short stay. He took my bag from me when he reached me and put his arm around my shoulders to steer me to the door.

"You look awfully green girl," he informed me as we stepped out into the stifling air once again.

"Nothing a little greasy food and a good night's sleep won't cure," I told him.

"That can be arranged."

On our way to the grounds he stopped at a small diner and ordered a dozen burgers and fries. When I raised my eyebrow at him he said the band would appreciate it after their sound check. As we headed out, bags in hand, he handed me a home-made strawberry milkshake for the road. I smiled at him and waved to the ladies behind the counter who had graciously helped us.

Fifteen minutes later we were pulling into the backside of the venue. We slowly made our way around numerous buses and campers, finally pulling to a stop in front of two buses parked side-by-side front to back so that the doors faced each other. Two large pop-up tents had been erected between them with picnic tables and chairs underneath. A few citronella candles were lit to ward off the evening bugs and their light bounced off the canopies above in the fading light of the day. It looked like a great place to spend a few days relaxing.

"Just leave your bag by that bus," Ace said gesturing with his elbow as his hands were full with the bags of food. "The guys should be back any time."

I dropped my bag where he told me to and moved to the picnic tables to help him. We had the food all spread out and Ace was just setting out an array of soda, beer and water on the table when the group showed up. Cort grabbed me before Knox had the chance and twirled me around. When he put me back on my feet he kissed me soundly on the lips, grinning at his brother.

"Enough," Knox growled coming up behind me and putting a hand on my hip.

He turned me around and before I could say hello he wrapped me in his arms and kissed me. It started out possessive to show his brother that I belonged to him, but when my knees buckled it became tender. I moaned when he pulled away causing him to chuckle and drop a light kiss on my nose. When his eyes narrowed and concern lined his face, I knew that he had seen the dark circles and the ashen color of my face.

"I'll be fine," I assured him. "I just need some food and a good night's sleep."

With that, he turned me and pushed me slightly towards the picnic tables. Ace moved over so I could sit and put a burger and fries on a plate for me. I thanked him and dug in. The guys started talking about the sound check and how excited they were that they were leading off in the morning that way they could have the rest of the festival to enjoy the show. That's when I noticed how gross they all were, covered in sweat and dust, yet how happy and relaxed they seemed. There was a different energy with this show compared to the other one that I had been to.

Once we were all done eating, a couple of the guys disappeared to shower, including Knox. It was a good chance for me to reacquaint myself with some of the other members of the band and they took full advantage of it by telling me all the embarrassing stories that they could about Knox since he couldn't defend himself. I laughed so hard I had tears streaming down my face. By the time he reappeared I was struggling to keep my eyes open, despite the fact that the guys still had me in stitches.

"Come on my girl," he whispered leaning down to gather me in his arms. "Let's get you to bed."

I didn't argue, snuggling into him and wrapping my arms around his neck. Closing my eyes, I trusted him to get me where I needed to be. The guys mumbled their good nights, but I barely heard them. I was starting to slip into slumber already. Next thing I knew I was being set on a soft bed and someone was removing my shoes. I attempted to lay back, yet was stopped when two large hands started pulling my dress over my head. My eyes popped open in alarm since I was disoriented.

"It's just me, baby" Knox crooned replacing my dress with one of his t-shirts.

The smell was comforting and helped drag me further under. With the feel of the bed underneath me I couldn't fight it any longer. Knox wrapped me in his arms again and moved me up the bed and under the covers. The minute my head hit the pillow I was officially out. I didn't even feel him crawl in or snuggle up next to me.

"Mmmmm," I purred stretching without opening my eyes the next morning.

I had been awake for some time just enjoying the feel of Knox's hands running up and down my sides and his lips nibbling their way down between my breasts to my naval and back. He clearly liked the movement I made because he used it to whip off my shirt and move himself completely between my legs. I felt him at the entrance to my body, though he still seemed in no rush to get there. He resumed nibbling and the feeling of his beard against my skin had me heating up and my core getting wetter.

I brought my hands down from above my head and threaded my fingers through his hair, directing his mouth to my breast. When he latched on, a zing went directly to my core. Rather than wait for him, I wrapped my legs around him and shifted to take him in. His erection was hard and pulsing. My body expanded to accommodate him and I let out a low moan of approval.

His hips slowly started to roll forward and away building friction between us. I locked my ankles around his lower back and dug my fingernails into his shoulders. I was only faintly aware of the fact that we weren't alone on the bus. I clenched my lips together tightly when he moved one of his hands down to rub gently on my clit igniting a whole other set of nerve endings. I increased the speed of my hips and I felt his chest vibrate from the groan he let out. Fusing our mouths together to muffle the noises, I felt myself on the brink of going over. Knox must have felt it as well because seconds later he had pulled completely out of my body and slammed into me. That was all it took for both of us.

"I could get used to waking up to that," I told him when I could breathe normally again.

"Me too," he whispered brushing the hair out of my face and placing a soft kiss on my nose.

"Maybe someday," I whispered back running my fingers through his hair.

"No maybe about it," he informed me. "Sooner rather than later, we will work something out so that we can spend more time together."

I pulled his mouth down to mine, feeling tears prick the backs of my eyes. Our tongues stroked each other gently and I felt him harden within me once again. I rocked slowly against him. Knox rolled over without breaking any contact putting his back on the bed and me above him. I straightened and he gripped my ass to move me on his shaft. I lifted my hands to my head and picked up my hair. I knew the angle would cause my boobs to bounce more with our movements and I felt him twitch inside me in response. Lifting onto my knees I came up off his member and dropped down again. He grunted and used his grip on my ass to repeat it a few more times. I was still sensitive enough that I felt the orgasm build before I could stop it. My insides clenching around him sent Knox right behind me.

"Can I ask you something?" I questioned some time later.

"Of course," he responded slipping from my folds and moving me so that we lay side by side.

"Do you want kids?" I asked nervously, biting my lip when his eyes got big. "Sorry! I knew it was too soon and especially not after sex."

"Slow down," he chuckled. "I do want kids. Where is this coming from though? I thought you wanted to wait awhile."

"I've been thinking about having my IUD taken out because they say you should give it some time once it does before you have children and I have already had it awhile. I'm not doing it necessarily for you," I yammered until he put his finger across my lips.

"I want kids and I would love to have them with you. My career is taking off though and I'm not sure if a baby is a good idea right now."

"I completely understand," I told him letting out a sigh of relief.

"For now, I need to get up and get outside. They start bringing around backstage winners early and I want to be out there to greet them."

Kicking him out of bed, I curled up and waited for the bathroom to be free. I felt so much better after broaching that subject with him as it has been on my mind a lot. I could wait to have kids, but I wasn't lying when I said I wanted to have the implement removed. At least I knew where he stood and it hadn't ended up being that big of a deal.

When he had finished and made his way to the front of the bus, I hopped in for a quick shower. Ten minutes later I was dressed in short jean shorts and a flowy top. I knew it would be hot and I wanted to be comfortable. I ran a quick brush through my damp hair and had just attached a baseball cap to one of my belt-loops when I heard voices outside the bus. Ace was saying something about breakfast and coffee. Before I had made it to the door I also heard female voices.

"You know, Knox, you look awfully lonely. If that girlfriend of yours isn't taking good care of you, I would be happy to step in."

"I think he's all set," I chuckled stepping out of the bus before Knox could say anything.

Both he and Ace lowered their eyes and stifled laughs. The woman who had voiced the invitation was a curvy girl in short shorts and a flannel sleeveless tied at the bottom. Her cheeks flared red and she stammered out an apology before fleeing with her friends to the camper on the other side of our buses. I made my way over to the picnic tables where Ace handed me a coffee in a travel mug with a large smile on his face.

"You know," Knox teased handing me a jelly filled donut, "you are going to scare away all my groupies."

I stuck my tongue out at him and sipped my drink. As we sat munching on our donuts and enjoying our coffee, multiple radio stations and their winners of backstage passes came by. Knox signed shirts, CDs, and pictures and chatted them up. Slowly other members of the band came out and grabbed breakfast. They were due to perform starting at nine o'clock that morning. Each singer/band would do two hours and there was an hour for lunch and an hour for dinner. The band would only be needed for the morning unless someone fell sick in another band and they filled in. Knox would hop on stage with a few others randomly during the day for some fun and surprise duets.

An hour or so before they were due to take the stage, Ace dropped a cord around my neck. I looked down and found a backstage pass laying against my chest. Playing with the plastic pass I smiled. It seemed I was an official groupie. Looking towards the bus I saw Knox coming out with a small backpack. When our eyes met he smiled from ear-to-ear and I couldn't have been more sure about my decision to come stay with him.

I got up to meet him and he handed me the bag, which was filled with water bottles and snacks. Ace, the band, Knox, and myself closed up the buses and headed to the stage. We hadn't walked far before Knox took my hand in his and interlaced our fingers. He waved, smiled, and nodded to others along our way, but I could feel the nerves he hid in his grip. I, on the other hand, was excited. I couldn't wait to see them on stage again.

When we arrived at the back of the stage we could already hear the gathering crowd. Knox released my hand as a woman with a headset came over to start hooking him up. Ace tugged me to his side as he gave last minute instructions to the guys. I smiled, my heart warm, when they gathered in a circle just before they took stage. Arms crossing over each other's shoulders they spoke in tones so low that only they could hear. Moments passed and they broke apart, smiles on all their faces and bouncing on the balls of their feet ready to perform. Knox jogged to me and gave me a chaste kiss before heading towards the entrance of the stage behind his band.

I followed Ace to a spot just off the side of the front of the stage. We could easily see the crowd and the performance. People were packed in. I had forgotten how many people came to Jamboree In The Hills and that it didn't matter what time the show was, it was filled to the hilt. I didn't see a bare spot on the hillside as I gazed around.

The opening strings to "Carnival" echoed around the field and the crowd started screaming. I couldn't keep my foot still and soon it was tapping along with the beat. Knox jumped up on the stage and started singing with energy that I still couldn't rival. They jumped from one song right into another. Four had passed before they took a break to interact with the crowd and for Knox to introduce the band.

My heart swelled with pride while I listened to him talk. I could completely understand his concern about the timing of a baby. He really was in his element on stage and his career was climbing day by day. I didn't want to take that from him, however, I did want to start planning for the future. When our eyes collided, I blew him a kiss and received a huge grin in return.

The days passed quickly, too quickly. Even though Knox had done some singing other than his own set, it had been a mini-vacation for him and the band. They were relaxed and recharged. Before I knew it, we were waking up on the final day. My plane flew out that evening, so I still had the whole day to spend with Knox, but I felt a sadness fill me nonetheless.

"It's way too early for that worry line to be creasing your beautiful face," Knox commented running his thumb across my brow.

"Just thinking about the fact that I have to leave you again," I told him lifting myself up to brace my chin on his chest and look at him.

"Stop thinking," he chided. "Or do I have to distract you again?"

I giggled and shook my head. We had been up for hours already and he had been "distracting" me plenty. I could hear people outside the bus starting their day and I had had to bite the pillow on the last round to keep everyone from hearing us. My body was so lax that I was pretty sure I couldn't stand even if I tried to roll out of bed at that moment. We could talk all day long when we were apart, yet get us together and we couldn't seem to keep our hands off each other.

"It just gets harder and harder to leave you," I whispered, my eyes filling with tears.

"Oh baby," he said pulling me up and tucking my head into the crook of his neck as he ran his hand up and down my bare back. "I wasn't kidding when I told you we would work something out. We just have to get through the rest of this tour."

"I know. I have plenty to keep me busy between signings, the book I am working on, and Kelly and Matt's wedding."

That's when I froze. He wouldn't be able to come to that. It was in September and he was going to be in the middle of his last leg. Plus, the wedding was on a weekend and 90% of his shows were on Friday and Saturday nights. I loved him more than I thought I could love a man, yet these were the times that I almost wished he was "normal".

"I'm sorry," he apologized kissing my head. "I promise you this will get easier. Just hold on a little bit longer, Kenzie."

"I'm holding, but you had better be worth it, cowboy," I half teased snuggling deeper into him and his comforting smell.

"I'm worth it and then some," he informed me once he had flipped me onto my back and I was looking up into his amazing brown eyes.

"I love you, Knox Pride," I whispered reaching my arms up around his neck.

"I love you too, Mackenzie Shaw," he whispered back, placing a soft kiss on my lips. "More than you know."

Chapter Fifteen

"Important events in our lives trigger us to want those that we love near, it seems to make them that much more special."

"Grrrrr," I growled rolling over yet again and putting my pillow over my head.

It was early, too early even for me, but I couldn't seem to go back to sleep. I had a feeling it was either all the writing I had been doing or the fact that I hadn't seen Knox in over a month. Everything seemed to be taking a toll on me. Sighing, I flopped onto my back and stared up at the ceiling. I refused to let myself be down and out.

I climbed out of bed and I made a quick bathroom stop before I headed downstairs. Starting my coffee, I fed the little boys that were weaving around my feet. I grabbed a banana muffin I had made the night before and when my coffee was ready I headed back upstairs. The horses were good for another couple of hours, so I figured I would get a little writing in.

I turned on my computer and sipped from my mug while I

waited for it to boot up. The little desk light allowed me to see my extra inventory books that lined my shelves causing me to smile. I was so lucky to be able to do what I absolutely loved for a living and the fact that people seemed to be enjoying it was just icing on the cake.

The book I was currently working on was flowing much quicker than any others I had done. Every time I sat down at the computer to work, my fingers would fly across the keys. I almost couldn't keep up with my thought process. It was amazing that it was that way even though I was struggling with the long-distance relationship thing. Usually if one thing in life was a little off balance I would struggle with my writing. This was not the case now.

A few hours later I was startled when a fresh cup of coffee appeared at my elbow along with another muffin. I wiped my eyes and shook my head to clear it. When I looked up I found Meghan grinning at me. I jumped up realizing I had been writing longer than I had planned and had yet to feed the horses. She quickly grabbed my shoulders and pushed me back down.

"You sit, drink your coffee and eat," she informed me. "I already took care of the boys outside."

"I'm so damn lucky to have you," I told her giving her a big hug and a sound kiss on the cheek.

"Glad you know it," she teased turning on her computer and grabbing her own mug that was sitting on her desk.

We worked the rest of the day in silence, the only noises in the office were those of us tapping on the keys. It was going to be a crazy week as we had to help Kelly with some last-minute wedding planning. Today was all about writing for me and social media and scheduling for Meghan. My phone going off in the bedroom across the hall was what finally broke our concentration.

I quickly saved what I was doing and ran to get it before it stopped ringing. I was hoping it was Knox since our connection time seemed less and less these days. I was mildly annoyed when it went silent by the time I got there and more so when I found that the caller had been Kelly and not my man. As much as I loved my future sister-in-law, she was in full bridezilla mode.

Dropping the phone in Meghan's lap on my way back into the office, I headed back to my computer to try to finish the chapter I was in the middle of. She laughed knowing my intent and called Kelly back. I blocked her out and let the flow come back to me.

"Should I take care of the boys before I go?" Meghan asked some time later, putting her hand on my shoulder to get my attention.

"Oh, is it that time already?"

"Yep," she chuckled. "I'll take care of the horses, but you need to make sure you stop to eat and feed the cats."

After a kiss on top of my head and a squeeze to my shoulder, she was gone. I worked for another hour, typing almost as fast as my brain was spitting out ideas. The cats knocking items off shelves finally interrupted my train of thought. It was their way of telling me that they were hungry. Shaking my head, I spoke to them and worked on saving and shutting down my computer.

Making my way downstairs, I was surprised to see how dark it was. I knew Meghan had said something about it being time to feed the horses, but I hadn't realized it was also past supper time. I fed the cats as they howled their disapproval for my being so late with their supper. I ran my hand down each of their backs once they were content and went to the fridge to find my own food.

My mom had obviously been in the house that afternoon.

On the second shelf sat a bowl of my favorite corn chowder with a note on how long to cook it and that there were biscuits in my breadbox on the counter. I silently thanked her and popped the container in my microwave. As it hummed along, I looked out the doors towards the pasture. The boys were cleaning up the rest of their meal and seemed perfectly content.

When I heard the d*ing* of the microwave signally that my supper was ready, I turned and a piece of paper caught my attention. I took my meal out and, once I checked it to see if it was warm enough, I moved back to the paper. It was a telephone number. Nick had made a delivery this week and had slipped his number into my hand when he had left. I took another bite and closed my eyes. He hadn't pushed, but had simply told me that he was interested if things didn't work out with Knox and me. The smile he had given me as he had climbed into his truck was enough to melt any woman, yet it hadn't done a thing for me. I had immediately felt guilty, even though I hadn't done anything wrong.

The little voice in the back of my mind decided then to speak up. *Wouldn't it be nice to date a man that lived closer? One that could be around for all the important things?* Opening my eyes, I let out a sigh. I loved Knox, that wasn't even a question, yet the distance thing was wearing me thin. Especially knowing my brother and Kelly were getting married in just a few weeks and he wouldn't be there as my date. Finishing my supper, I put the phone number in the trash and shut off the lights. It was time for bed and for my brain to turn off.

"Okay, next," the beautician Jaime signaled for Alicia to get out of the chair and for me to climb in.

It was the day of my brother's wedding and I wasn't sure who was more nervous, his future wife or myself. Three mimosas later we had all calmed down a bit and it was just the two of us, Kelly and I, left to have our hair done. In just a few hours she would go from being my friend to being my sister. I was so happy for the two of them.

"So, you're the one who was supposedly dating Knox Pride, huh?" Jaime's assistant asked as she broke open another container of bobby pins.

"Was supposedly?" I asked, barely holding back a laugh.

"Someone said that you were, but I just saw this article in a magazine of him and another woman," she informed me handing me the article. "So, my guess is that he has moved on."

I rolled my eyes at the girls sending them all into fits. As Jaime worked on putting large wavy curls into my hair, I looked at the magazine. Sure enough the article showed a picture of Knox and another woman, Angela, to be exact. Based on the clothes, I could tell the picture was an old one. Meghan grabbed it from me and laughed out loud when she saw it.

"Yeah," I told the assistant with a smile. "I'm the one who was supposedly dating Knox."

When our hair was done the four of us climbed into Alicia's SUV and headed to my parents' house. The wedding and reception were both being held outside in the backyard. The old barn out back had also been cleaned out to be used as a dance floor or just a place to hang out should we need it. Pulling into the driveway, I hopped out first to make sure the guys were still getting ready in the game room above the garage so that Matt wouldn't see Kelly before the ceremony.

I didn't get far when I saw Brandon in the window. He gave me a thumbs up and I motioned for the girls to hurry up and get out. We all headed upstairs to what had been my bedroom growing up, now it was my mother's office. It wasn't an easy trip considering the house was buzzing between family and wedding people. Our dresses hung along the folding closet doors when we entered causing us to stop and join hands.

While the four of us had come from neighboring towns with absolutely nothing in common, we had somehow formed a kinship that had spanned over a decade. Squeezing Kelly and Meghan's hands I felt my eyes well up. This was the first big life event for our group and we were all feeling a little emotional.

"Time to get dressed," Alicia stated letting go of our hands and clapping hers together. "If we stand here much longer we are going to ruin our make-up."

Smiling we agreed and got moving. Minutes later Meghan, Alicia, and myself were clad in our burgundy floor length dresses. Meghan's had simple large straps at the top, Alicia's was a halter, and mine had one shoulder strap. The material was silky, form fitting, and gorgeous. While the others finished fussing over their dresses I snapped a quick selfie in the full-length mirror and sent it to Knox.

"Missing your man?" Kelly asked putting her head on my shoulder and looking at me in the mirror.

"Yeah, a little, but this is your day," I informed her putting my hand on her arm. "And it's time to get you in your dress."

Alicia took my signal to take the wedding dress down from where it was hanging. The three of us gathered around to help her get into it. A ton of giggling later, we had her zipped in. The dress was a strapless with a heart cut and millions of little sequins. It came down to a slight flare and rustled as she moved. I rolled my eyes up to keep them from filling up again. Jess, the photographer, snapped away without ever bothering us. When Kelly's parents came in and started gushing over her I grabbed my shoes and slipped out for a few minutes.

Making my way down the stairs I found my mother hovering over the caterers. The two of us made sure everything was all set to go. The chairs were filling up quickly with guests and Matt, Brandon, Nick, and Matt's friend Alec, were milling about chatting with people. They were all dressed in tuxes with burgundy vests and ties that matched perfectly to our dresses. My brother looked so handsome and happy. I felt my eyes start to fill and shifted them to the ceiling once again.

"Almost time to start," my mom stated looking at the clock. "Why don't you go get the girls moving and I'll go get those boys up to the front."

Nodding, I kissed her on the cheek and headed back upstairs. Kelly's mother and the other two girls went back down first. Kelly's father slipped out next leaving us alone. I fidgeted with her dress and made sure her hair and vail were just so. Without saying a word, I kissed her and joined our hands. We walked out of the room together gripping each other tightly.

The ceremony went by in a blur and before I knew it we were heading back down the aisle behind my brother and his new wife. I squeezed Brandon's arm and he covered my hand with his. It was hard to believe that at one point I had thought this was what he and I were headed for. Now, I took comfort in the fact that we had gotten back the friendship we had had growing up.

We followed Kelly, Matt, and Jess out to the field behind the barn for pictures. A half hour later we were making our way to the head table amongst cheers from all the guests. The caterer didn't give us a chance to sit down before he was waving us over to start a line. Despite the country setting, Kelly had wanted an elaborate set up, food, and the men in tuxes. She had gotten everything she dreamed of.

Once dinner was over and the plates cleared away it was time for the first dance. Meghan, Alicia, and I sat hand in hand while we watched the two move around the floor as husband and wife. Now that pictures were done, tears flowed freely down our cheeks. I missed Knox more than ever at that moment, not just because he was missing it but because this was what I dreamed of having with him. I wanted it so badly it physically hurt.

Soon, we were all out on the dance floor. The beat had picked up and the four of us instantly found each other when one of our favorite songs from high school came on. Singing with our hands in the air, I was unbelievably content. When the beat finally slowed down I shifted to step off the floor, yet found myself face-to-face with Nick, my brother's groomsman and the same man who had left me his number.

"May I have this dance?" he asked putting his hand out.

"Of course," I responded putting mine in his and following him back out to the crowd.

I put my left hand on his shoulder and my right in his left. Alicia raised her eyebrows at me from where she was dancing with her fiancé and Meghan had an "O" shape to her mouth from where she was standing off to the side with her drink. I rolled my eyes at them and moved with the music.

"Kelly did an amazing job with everything," he commented pulling me a little bit closer to him.

"She did," I agreed. "She had such a distinct picture in her head and I think she accomplished it."

"Do you?" he asked.

"Have a picture of my dream wedding?"

"Yeah."

"I thought I did," I told him honestly. "However, I think it has changed a bit since I have gotten involved with Knox."

I felt him stiffen under my fingertips and instantly felt bad. I knew Nick was interested, but I had made it quite clear that I was taken. When he had handed me his number I had given him a look and he had simply shrugged and handed it to me anyway. I leaned my head back to look at him out of the corner of my eye. He was a good-looking guy. Well-built with blue eyes and jet black hair. He also had a tattoo that covered one upper arm and shoulder, at least from what I had seen. If I hadn't already been involved, he would have been just what I would have been attracted to.

"Mind if I cut in?" I heard a voice ask from behind me.

Nick's arms immediately released me and I turned to find myself looking into my favorite pair of brown eyes. Knox had made it. He was dressed in dark grey slacks and a black button-up dress shirt. I couldn't help the smile that split my face. My dance partner stepped aside graciously and I was gathered up in the solid warm arms of my boyfriend.

"I thought you had a concert last night and tomorrow?" I whispered in his ear in disbelief.

"I did. I do," he replied into mine. "But I knew this was important to you so I wanted to be here."

I kissed his neck and held onto him tightly. Those words were just what I needed to hear. All the worries I had had the past few days went out the window. Unfortunately, the song was over much too quickly and we separated. Intertwining our fingers, he led me off the dance floor and around the side of the barn.

We got out of the view of everyone and I felt the barn at my back. I was pinned by a solid body and my mouth was quickly consumed in a hot kiss that had my toes curling in my strappy shoes. My hands knotted in the front of his shirt and my nipples perked against the front of my dress.

"You look gorgeous," Knox gasped when he pulled away. "I figured this was more appropriate than dragging you back to your house to have my way with you."

"We can do that later," I informed him as I ran my hands down his shirt and gently brushed over the front of his pants.

"Evil woman," he hissed stepping back a bit. "Now we have to wait longer before we go back out there."

"Thank you for coming," I said turning somber.

"I love you," he stated simply, cupping my cheek. "I will be here for you whenever it is humanly possible."

"I love you too."

"Now, let's get out there so I can remind all those men that you are taken."

Chapter Sixteen

"Halloween allows people to hide behind masks and mistaken identities, costumes can allow us to have a confidence we might not otherwise have."

F all was in full swing and usually it was my favorite season. This year, unfortunately, I was just ready for it to be over, which was turning me grumpier by the moment. Meghan and I even butted heads enough that she took a couple days off to get away from me. I knew what my problem, or problems were, I just couldn't seem to pull myself out of it.

Seeing Knox at Kelly and Matt's wedding had basically set things off. He had shown up later in the afternoon and had only been able to stay until early the next morning. Though I was grateful for the little bit of time, it had felt like a tease. I had also had my IUD removed, leaving me feeling nervous and a little unsure. My hormones were clearly not happy with the shift. To top it all off I had booked multiple local craft fairs along with book signings so I felt stretched too thin. Never mind the fact that Knox was finishing up his tour causing him to be extremely exhausted and punchy when we did talk.

"This is not helping," I mumbled rubbing my temples to ease the pain behind them.

"What's up?" Meghan asked, turning in her chair.

It was the first day she had been back since our tiff and we were both treading lightly around each other. This was one of the reasons hiring your friends could be difficult. The two of us had always been strong willed and had often disagreed, yet this revolved around my livelihood so I was much more sensitive.

"Writer's block. Headache."

"I'm sorry, hon," she sympathized coming over to rub my shoulders.

"So frustrating," I moaned crossing my arms on my desk and plopping my head down on top of them.

"Sounds to me like you need a break," she advised digging her thumbs into my shoulder blades. "Maybe you should go see Knox."

"I can't," I mumbled, tears instantly pricking my eyes. "He is on screech finishing the tour and he is exhausted."

"Hmmm," I heard her respond as my eyes fluttered shut.

I felt my back and neck muscles start to release under her fingers. Letting my mind clear, I stretched my back out and made myself more comfortable. Meghan worked her way from my neck down to my lower back. By the time she was done I felt like mush and was on the verge of napping.

"Go lay down for a bit," she finally said, gripping my arm and helping me up. "I know you haven't been sleeping."

"Just for a little while. Don't let me sleep late, otherwise I won't tonight."

Three hours later the alarm on my phone woke me up. Turning over, I shut it off and climbed out of my cocoon. When I made my way into the office, my friend was nowhere to be seen, but she had left a folder with a note in the middle of my desk. Getting closer, it read:

Ace and my present for you and Knox.

-<3-

Meghan

I opened the folder to find an itinerary for a Halloween trip to Nashville along with an invitation for Knox's family's annual party. Under that paperwork sat an order printout for a costume purchase. I smiled and sighed. I was so grateful that they had done this for us, but I really hoped they had talked to Knox. His tour ended the week before the party and I knew that he was looking forward to some quiet time with his family.

Closing the folder, I sent Meghan a quick text thanking her. Before I even made it downstairs, I received a *"You're welcome"* response, quickly followed by a *"Knox doesn't know, but Ace assured me he wanted you there. Enjoy!"* I laughed, making my way to the kitchen to feed the cats and take care of the boys outside. My heart swelled. I would see him again soon and I would get to spend four full days with him. I couldn't wait.

"Are you ever going to get off the plane and not be green?" Ace asked me as he grabbed my bag from the carousel at the airport two weeks later.

"I would have been fine if it hadn't been for all the damn turbulence," I mumbled hoping my stomach contents stayed where they were.

"I'll get you some of your greasy food and I'll get you to the room so you can nap," he told me as we made our way out to the truck.

"You take such good care of me."

"Anything for Knox's girl. Your family," he stated matter-of-factly.

"Does he know?" I asked making myself comfortable when he pulled out into traffic.

"Nope. He has been moping, just like you from what I hear."

"I have not been moping. Struggling creatively is my problem."

"Sure," he chuckled.

When we got to the hotel I was surprised to see it was the same one that Knox and I had stayed at for the awards show. Ace took the larger of my two bags and led the way inside. The ladies at the front desk greeted us like old friends and while he checked in I pulled out my cell. Knox was blowing it up with *I love you*s and *I miss you*s causing me to smile.

"That the man?" Ace asked signaling for me to follow him.

"Yep, I'm afraid to answer or say too much," I admitted, getting into the elevator behind him.

"You two are ridiculous," he teased.

I stuck my tongue out at him and was rewarded with a smile. When the elevator stopped, I was astonished to see that we were on the same floor and going to the same suite as before. I raised my eyebrows at Ace only to receive a shrug. Following him in, I dropped my bag and collapsed on the couch.

"The party is at seven at Cash's. I've ordered you room service so after you eat you'll have some time to nap."

"Perfect. Thank you so much," I said getting up to hug him before he left.

It wasn't fifteen minutes after he left that there was a knock on the door and my food was delivered. I quickly gobbled it down to ease my cramping stomach. After, I set the alarm on my phone so I could nap and have plenty of time to get ready. With the warm full feeling in my belly, I snuggled deep into the large bed and crashed.

"Did Ace tell her we were coming?" I heard a voice whisper loudly.

"Probably not, knowing him," another answered.

I flopped over and opened my eyes slowly. Stretching, I sat up and looked at the women whose voices had woken me up. The same two that had helped me to get ready before, Lexie and Casey, stood at the end of the bed grinning at me. I gave them a mock glare and reached back to grab and silence my phone.

"Come on girl," Lexie boomed. "Let's get you sexier than you already are."

Rolling my eyes, I untangled myself from the blankets and climbed out of bed. Before I jumped in the shower, I pulled my costume out and hung it up eliciting a low whistle from both girls. It was definitely a more provocative outfit than I would normally wear. Knox was going as a pirate, so Meghan had picked out something between a female pirate and a bar wench. There was a low cut red and black corset top with black sheer sleeves. The short skirt was sheer black as well and I had matched it with fishnet stockings and thigh high boots.

As soon as I was clean and wrapped in a robe both ladies got to work. This time Lexie curled my entire head in long waves and pinned it all up on top leaving only a few stray tendrils to escape. She spent more time on my make-up than she had the last time, leaving me a little uneasy to go to the mirror. She wouldn't let me look until I had the entire outfit on. Once I had gotten dressed, the three of us stood in front of the full-length mirror with our mouths open.

"Wow!" I exclaimed. "How do you do that?"

"You're gorgeous to begin with," Lexie complimented, "so it doesn't take much."

With that the two packed up and left. My eyes were done dark, yet they demanded your attention and the slight pink powder on my cheeks instantly drew your gaze to the deep red she had painted my lips. I was a beautiful woman; however, I had never been able to do my make-up the way she did. Ten minutes later when Ace came in and let out a long whistle, I blushed.

"That man is damn lucky he hooked you first," Ace said with a chuckle and a wink.

"Thanks, I think I've heard that before," I replied with a laugh.

I didn't bother grabbing items from my purse since my drinks were free and they knew who I was. Ace grabbed the bags that I had repacked and we headed out. The drive was short, but I was extremely nervous and wrung my hands the entire way there. When we pulled around to the back and parked by the entrance to the apartment I let out the breath I had been holding.

The costume made me feel sexy and powerful despite the butterflies wreaking havoc in my stomach. As we rounded the front of the building I caught several pairs of eyes on me from the men waiting to get in, bringing Ace in closer and his hand to the small of my back. I grinned while he nodded to the security and we went inside.

For a family party, the place was packed. We made our way towards the bar, my protector still standing close. My heart picked up pace when I caught sight of Knox through the crowd. A pirate he was, in a large hat, billowing white shirt and leather pants; he could steal any woman's breath away. My stomach threatened to send dinner back up when I saw him talking to a woman in a revealing nurse's uniform. She was as near as he would allow with one hand on his muscular forearm and the other toying with her hair. I felt Ace tense as we approached. I looked up to Knox's face and was relieved when I saw that he was merely tolerating her and that his eyes were screaming *Save me!*

"Ace, it's about time you got here," Knox boomed, turning away from the nurse and grabbing his friend. "Who's your date?"

Just after he questioned him, his eyes locked with mine. The surprise was evident and his breathing seemed to catch as he took me in, head to toe. His smile and a slight shift of his hips showed his appreciation. Before he could step towards me, the woman still at his elbow decided that she didn't like being ignored and gripped him.

"I've missed you, baby girl," he drawled with a shake to dislodge her and a move to gather me in his arms.

I barely heard her cry of dismay or Ace's move to intercept her coming at us. Knox gathered me up for a two second hug and the next thing I knew he was dragging me across the floor towards the bathrooms. Getting around people wasn't easy, but the man was on a mission. As we entered the hallway that housed the restrooms I realized that he was actually headed to a door beyond them. Opening it, he pulled me in.

I was slammed against the door and, just before Knox's mouth came crashing down on mine, I heard the click of the lock. I met him lick for lick as his tongue invaded my mouth. His erection was against my lower belly and I moaned when he pushed his hips into mine seductively. The sounds coming from me must have set him off further because I heard the sounds of his zipper and a condom wrapper being opened. His mouth never left mine, only increasing the speed of his tongue as he rolled on the protection.

I felt one of his hands slide up my thigh under my skirt and I grinned against his mouth when his fingertips met mostly skin around my thong. The growl he released rumbled from deep within him and I brought one leg up to bring him closer to my core and wrap around his hip. Both of his hands grabbed my ass and lifted me. Almost losing my balance, I wrapped my arms around his neck and moved my mouth to the spot just below his ear as he penetrated me in one quick thrust.

The friction had me crying out and my insides clenching around him. He moved in and out a few times increasing the intensity. When he brought one hand around to my front and gently flicked my clit I was pushed over the edge. While my insides milked his member, he covered my mouth with his and followed suit.

Still holding me, Knox gently brought my legs down and my feet to the floor as he pulled out. He disposed of the condom and gently tucked himself back into his pants. Leaning on the door, my legs still shaking, something dawned on me.

"Why were you carrying a condom?" I asked, my voice wavering from the sudden fear of what his answer would be.

"I wasn't," he stated uneasily, turning slightly to point at the open desk drawer behind him. "The guys keep a box in here."

I slumped against the door slightly and closed my eyes to keep them from filling with tears. Feeling Knox move closer to me, I tensed. Relaxing slightly when I felt him wiping my inner thigh with what smelled like a baby wipe, I tried to control my raging emotions. I hated that I immediately thought the worst and that seeing him with another woman had made me feel slightly unsure. After some rustling around, I felt his warm hands cup my cheeks.

"Kenz, I need you to open your eyes and look at me."

His pleading tone had my eyelids lifting. Brown eyes searched blue ones. I didn't know what to say to him. Knox's handsome face had confusion written all over it, but a closer look showed a hint of fear as well. I covered his hands with my own and took a shaky breath.

"I would never cheat on you," he informed me with a slight catch in his words. "If I was that unhappy, I would tell you."

"I know," I whispered.

"But if you want something else you need to let me know," he stated leaning his forehead against mine. "I know I'm not an easy man to love."

"On the contrary, Knox, you're a very easy man to love," I told him with a laugh. "You are putting a damper on my writing though."

"I love you, baby girl," he replied with a relieved grin.

"I love you, too," I said squeezing his hands and running them down the front of his shirt to rest on his hips. "I'm sorry that seeing you with that woman set me off."

"Jealous?" he teased.

"Hell yeah. How could I not be?"

"Good because I was too," he let me know as he released me to clean up the mess he had made with the desk. "Why do you think I dragged you in here? Between you dancing with that guy at the wedding and seeing you with Ace tonight."

I raised my eyebrows at him with a sly smile on my face. He shook his head as he finished putting things back in the drawer and straightening up the papers on top. While he did that, I assessed the damage to my costume and my make-up. The clothes were fine, but I did need to reapply my lipstick. I searched around in my cleavage to find the emergency stick Casey had given me and used a little mirror on the wall to touch it up. With a touch or two to my hair, I turned back to Knox to receive a low whistle and found him looking at me with lust-filled eyes.

Grabbing his hand and tugging, I steered him towards the door, "Let's go show all those women you're taken."

Chapter Seventeen

"An engagement ring symbolizes a never-ending promise of love, the sight of it on a woman's finger can still excite her years in the future."

CLOP! CRUNCH! CLOP! CRUNCH!

The sounds of Max's feet in the leaves relaxed me and reminded me of why I had horses in the first place. They were great therapy when the world got to be too much. Today was one of those days. I had been running around so much between housework, signings, and craft fairs that I hadn't had much time for myself lately. Knox was due in at some point that day and I had decided riding was better than sitting around the house going crazy.

We had seen each other two weeks ago for a long weekend, but this time we would spend a whole week together. It would be the longest stretch yet and to say I was a little nervous was an understatement. I was worried that the more time we spent together that we would figure out we wouldn't work as a couple. Not to mention that we had slipped up last weekend and had forgotten a condom. It was only once, but that was all it took.

"Okay, boy," I cooed to the chestnut beneath me. "Let's go!"

The horse had picked up on my desire to run some of my jumpiness out and I had been holding him back until we had moved into a sheltered field on my family's property. He easily picked through his gears and was galloping full out before I knew it. Instead of fear, exuberance flowed through me. There was nothing like the wind in your hair, the power of an animal between your legs, and the sound of their feet steadily hitting the ground.

When we approached the tree line, I reigned him in and with a toss of his head he complied. I scratched his neck and murmured *good boy* to him when he quickly quieted down. We plodded along the trails and I took deep breaths to fill my lungs with cool air. It was the perfect fall day in Maine.

Almost two hours later we rode back through the field behind my barn. I noticed a truck in the driveway and my heart sped up. It looked like Knox had arrived early. When we drew up to the gate to let us back in to the pasture, I was surprised to find Brandon standing there to open it for us. Panic immediately set in.

"Brandon?" I greeted, a question in my tone.

"Everything is fine," he informed me. "Well, for you any way."

I breathed a sigh of relief and directed Max to head for the gate to the barn. I heard our visitor come up behind us as I hopped off the horse's back. He didn't say anything, he just came up and unlatched the gate motioning for me to go in. I followed his lead and got Max settled in to the cross ties before turning back to him.

Brandon sat in one of the lawn chairs lining the alley of the barn. His head was in his hands. Between the slump of his shoulders and his face, he looked defeated. I moved to him and put my hand on his shoulder to get him to look up at me.

"What's going on?"

"Emmy kicked me out," he finally whispered. "We had a huge fight."

I stepped back as though I'd been burned. Granted the two of us had been friends longer than we had been in a relationship, but he had cheated on me with this woman. He had gotten her pregnant and had a baby. Now he expected me to comfort him? Was he crazy?

"I guess I deserve that," he muttered shaking his head and getting up to pace.

"You can understand my abundance of sympathy," I uttered sarcastically as I went back to Max to finish untacking him.

"I'm sorry for what I did to you," he apologized, coming to stand on the other side of my horse as I undid the knot in my leather and released the girth.

"I'm not," I told him honestly. "However, it is a little awkward that you would come to me when you start having relationship problems with her."

"You've always been the person I turned to for this kind of thing," he argued moving around to stand beside me as I put my saddle on the floor.

"That was before we had a relationship," I informed him. "Before we had slept together."

"I don't know who else to turn to."

He totally blew the wind out of my sails with that one. I totally understood. Brandon was an only child and hadn't been particularly close to his divorced parents. He had spent more time with our family growing up than he had his own. I sighed and looked up at him when he put his hands on my shoulders.

"What did you do now?" I asked with a light grin.

"I may have said some things I didn't mean after too many beers," he admitted, not yet releasing me.

"Like what kinds of things?"

"I may have possibly compared her to you and may have commented that I was stupid for giving you up," he said, slowly enunciating each word.

"You are an idiot!" I exclaimed trying to pull away from him.

"I didn't mean it," he replied holding me still so he could look me in the eye. "I love her and Mikey more than anything. I panicked when she started talking about this guy that she is working with.

"Again, you're an idiot," I repeated staring at him.

"What do I do, Mackenzie?" he whimpered.

"You grovel. A lot. You apologize and you offer her everything under the sun," I told him reaching up to squeeze his hands with mine. "And you never use my name like that again or tell her you ask me for relationship advice."

"That's it? I don't know if she will even let me back into the house."

"Bud, she loves you. She'll let you in, just let her cool down for a bit."

I felt him relax his hands and watched as he let out a long shaking breath. I smiled, he really did care about this woman and I couldn't have been happier for him despite the circumstances. We weren't meant to be a couple. Emmy was his other half the same way Knox was mine. Suddenly, all the stress surrounding me about my relationship drained away.

"Thank you," he said kissing me on the forehead. "You always know how to make me feel better."

"Sorry for interrupting," came a familiar voice from behind me.

I immediately turned around and cringed internally when I saw the hurt on Knox's face. I pulled out from under Brandon's hands and moved to embrace my boyfriend, only to be stopped by his hand coming up. I froze and my heart nearly broke when he took a step back.

"I'll see you in the house when you're done," he mumbled, his voice barely a whisper.

Fear instantly gripped my chest. I took a step back, leaning into Max, and wiped my hands down my face. This couldn't be happening. I had seen thousands of women throw themselves at Knox and I had had to accept it. Now, one innocent scene had him pulling away. I didn't think so.

"Oh Kenz, I'm so sorry," Brandon started.

I cut him off with one hand while I used the other to brush down my horse. Pointing towards the door, I didn't say a word. There weren't any. My emotions were boiling too close to the surface and I wouldn't take them out on him.

He seemed to understand and with a nod started by me. Stopping briefly to squeeze my shoulder, he let himself out of the barn through the tack room. By the time Max was cleaned up and I was unclipping the cross ties, Brandon had started his truck and was pulling down the driveway.

I latched the gate and leaned on it as I watched Max amble over to where his brothers were nibbling at the nonexistent grass on the ground. I knew I was stalling, but I was nervous about what I would find when I went in. Would he decide that we were over and leave? Would we fight and work through it? It could go either way considering that up to this point our relationship had been fairly carefree.

Sighing, I closed the overhead door and put my brush tote and my tack back where they belonged. After sweeping the alleyway, I realized I couldn't put it off any longer and headed to the house. Opening the sliding glass door, I slipped in and found Knox leaning on the island with both hands looking at a ring box. I shut the door and pulled my boots off before moving to stand in front of him with the counter between us.

"Do you know part of the reason I came here this week?" he asked after we had stood there in silence for a while.

"I can take a guess," I replied gesturing towards the box.

"I have spent so much time planning the right words to say to you, how to do it, whether or not to include your family," he explained, reaching out to open the box and place it facing me. "But now I battle with the fact that you deserve something better. Someone that can be here for you all the time and that you don't have to spend so much time chasing across the country."

Tears filled my eyes and I brought my hands up to cover my mouth. The ring was radiant cut with a gold band and had to be almost two carats. A matching wedding band sat beside it that was encrusted with alternating diamonds and sapphires, which were Knox's birthstone. It was the most beautiful set I had ever seen. My eyes came up to connect with his and saw so much brewing behind those brown orbs. I wasn't giving this man up without a fight, ring or not.

"Do you know what I was doing out there?" I asked him, rhetorically speaking, and walking around the island. "I was comforting a friend. I was also realizing that all the crap, the travel, the FaceTimes, the late-night calls, they are all worth it if it means I get to have you."

Knox turned to me and cupped my face in his hands while mine found his hips. He seemed more relaxed once I had said my piece and his eyes had filled with unshed tears. He smiled at me before placing a couple of soft sweet kisses on my lips. I returned the smile and brought my hand up to wipe away the tears that were tracking down his face.

"That night just over a year ago at Cash's I knew you were

special, though I didn't realize just how much you would come to mean to me or how quickly. I'm pretty sure I fell in love with you when we danced and you knew who I was, yet you didn't make a big deal of it," he informed me circling his thumbs on my cheeks. "You are everything to me, Mackenzie Shaw, and I would be the happiest man alive if you would do me the honor of becoming my wife."

I nodded, tears now streaming down my own face, unable to speak. Knox gathered me in his arms and I held on tightly. When we finally parted, he reached around me to grab the box. He pulled out the engagement ring and put it on my left hand. It fit perfectly. I looked at him in confusion.

"I called your parents," he said with a shrug. "Did you honestly think I would do this without asking your father first?"

"Have I told you how much I love you?" I asked kissing him.

"No, but you can sure as hell show me," he answered with a sly grin.

We spent the next three days celebrating, just the two of us, as well as getting used to "living" together. It also gave us some time to figure out the important things that came with marriage, like housing and kids. I was relieved when we agreed that my place would be our home base and when we traveled to Nashville that we would either stay with his parents or at his apartment, much like we already did. It wasn't going to be easy, but it would definitely be worth it.

Thanksgiving morning, I got up early to start the turkey and treated myself to climbing back in bed with Knox for an hour. I only had to make a couple of pies since everyone would bring a couple dishes with them of sides and other desserts. We would have a full house with my parents, Kelly and Matt, Alicia and her fiancé Devon, Meghan, and Brandon, Emmy, and Mikey. I couldn't wait to share our news with them officially. We had told Knox's family the night before while Face-Timing with Cort.

"We're here! You had better be decent!" we heard Matt yell hours later as the family started to filter through the front door.

Knox kissed my cheek and with a nervous smile went to help everyone. He had admitted to me that he was worried about my family and friends thinking we had gotten engaged too fast, despite the fact that my parents had graciously given him their approval. I finished cleaning up so there would be room for all the crockpots and sides on the counter. I glanced at my ring quickly and couldn't stop the grin that formed on my lips.

"Happy Thanksgiving!" my mom greeted coming into the kitchen first.

I ran around the island to grab her in a one arm hug and take the bowl of squash from her hands. The room became pure pandemonium as everyone seemed to come in at once. Hugs and kisses were exchanged and plates, bowls, and slow cookers were arranged on the counter. Knox stood off to the side taking it all in and we shared a smile across the room.

"Oh my God! Is that what I think it is?" Kelly gasped holding my hand up for inspection.

I grinned like a fool and tears pricked my eyes as I nodded. I had hugged her last and no one else had noticed, however when our hands had come down from the exchange our rings had hit catching her attention. Alicia and Meghan quickly joined our huddle to look as well. When Kelly finally looked up I was unsure what I would see. All three of them started squealing and pulled me in for a group hug. I was so relieved and glad that they were happy for me.

I felt a large warm hand on my back and expected to see Knox, but instead it was my dad. His smile was sad and elated all at the same time and tears were coming down his face.

Seeing that set me off and I jumped into his arms. I heard the others around us congratulating my future husband and didn't pull away from my father until my brother broke in looking much like my dad had. I grabbed Matt and hugged him for all I was worth. We were only a few years apart and had always been close, however, I had never seen him get emotional when it came to me.

Ten minutes later when everyone was done hugging, kissing, and crying, we started grabbing plates and digging in. I didn't have enough room at my table for everyone, however we made do with those we could fit there and also with the island. It was squishy, loud, and perfect. I couldn't have been happier. My world was surrounding me, my friends, family, and Knox. I looked around and took in all of them chatting and smiling. Feeling a hand on my thigh, I covered it with my own and looked into the eyes of the man that would soon be my husband. He leaned in and gave a sweet kiss.

"Happy Thanksgiving, baby girl," he whispered for my ears only.

"Happy Thanksgiving, handsome."

Chapter Eighteen

"There is nothing like having your family around you when it means the most, celebrating with them is the best possible party."

"Oh no!" I gasped looking at the stick again. "This can't be right!"

Placing it back on the counter, next to three just like it, I guess it couldn't be wrong. I was pregnant. Sitting on the side of the tub, I covered my face with my hands and took a couple of deep breaths. They say all it takes is once. Well, that was all it took. That one time back in November before Thanksgiving when we had rushed things without thinking, without using any protection.

A small smile crept onto my face. I was a little excited. This had been what I had wanted all along: marriage and a baby with the man that I loved. Timing was far from perfect, especially with both of our busy schedules, but we would make it work. I immediately looked down at the ring that Knox had put on my finger just a few weeks ago and I froze.

Both of the conversations that we had had in regards to kids had ended with him being very adamant about waiting. With the crazy touring schedule he would have the next couple of years, as well as recording, he didn't want us to have that added responsibility. I got it, I really did, yet the happiness crept back in. I got up and quickly snapped a picture on my phone before placing all the tests in one of the drawers.

I avoided Knox's phone calls because I knew that if I actually talked to him I would tell him the news. I had even gone so far as to try to deter him from coming for Christmas. I didn't know what to do. I needed more time and he would be here Christmas Eve which was less than a week away. The doctor's office had had a cancellation so they had been able to get me in for an appointment with my doctor and for a quick ultrasound. At least going to that would give me the confirmation I needed.

"Mackenzie Shaw," the nurse called stepping into the waiting room.

I waved at her and got up to follow her through the door and back to where the exam rooms were. I saw a couple of the girls at the receptionist desk look at me and talk amongst themselves. I knew that doctors had a confidentiality agreement due to doctor patient privilege, but did that extend to all staff? I sure hoped so as I stepped on the scale for her to record my weight. I didn't need this getting out to the public before I told Knox or the rest of my family.

Once we went through all the basics, blood pressure, medications, history, etc., she left me to change into a gown. I did so and climbed up onto the table to wait for my doctor. I couldn't stop wringing my hands or playing with my ring. My nerves started to get the best of me at the same time there was a light knock and the door opened slightly.

"Well, hello there," my doctor greeted as she came in,

closing the door, and moving to settle on the rolling stool in front of the computer.

"Hi Pam," I returned letting out a shaky breath.

"So, what's going on? You weren't due in for another year," she commented signing in to the computer and looking from the screen in front of her to me.

"I think I'm pregnant," I told her gripping my hands together again.

"You think?" she chuckled.

"Well four tests say I am," I replied giving her a weak smile.

"Okay. Lean back, put your feet up, and let's take a look."

Forty-five minutes later I was sitting in my vehicle, crying large alligator tears, staring at an ultrasound picture of my baby. I was so happy, yet so scared all at the same time. Every time I reached to pick up my phone and call Knox to tell him the news I would cry again. This was something I had to share with him in person, I just didn't know how he would take it.

The next few days I avoided the girls feigning the flu and even tried again to get Knox to hold off on visiting. He argued with me and said that if I was sick he wanted to come and take care of me. My appetite started to decrease and I wondered if I really was getting sick or if it was the pregnancy. I finally came to the conclusion that it probably had a bit to do with the little human growing inside me as well as nerves.

"Yeah, yeah," I mumbled making my way back from the barn to the house through the freshly fallen snow. "I know you're hungry."

I had spent a couple of hours brushing down the boys while they enjoyed a light breakfast before turning them out with the rest of their hay. After they were settled, I had cleaned the barn and their stalls. I was long past my normal breakfast time and I felt nausea starting to build. I knew better. It hadn't taken me long to figure out that I needed to have food in my stomach at all times otherwise I would feel sick. I hadn't physically gotten sick yet, but it had threatened pretty strongly a couple of times.

Letting myself into the kitchen, I took off my boots and made tracks to make a cup of hot chocolate and to start my toast. Once it was done I grabbed my cup and my peanut butter toast and made my way to the living room. A good Christmas Hallmark movie was calling my name. I was startled when I got closer to the front door and Knox's travel bag was sitting there.

Confused, I rounded the corner into the living room and found my fiancé asleep on the couch. I put my stuff down on the side table by my recliner and walked over to sit down on the coffee table directly in front of the couch. My movements never woke him, so I knew he had to be exhausted. I racked my brain trying to figure out if I had totally lost track of my days and it was Christmas Eve or if he had come early as he said he would. I pulled out my phone and confirmed it, he had come to take care of me.

Sighing, I watched him as he slept. His features were peaceful. One arm was slung over his head and one leg was bent at the knee with his work booted foot on the floor. I couldn't help but reach out and run a finger gently down his bearded jawline to where I knew his dimple would be if he smiled. Panic suddenly hit me like a ton of bricks. What was I going to do?

"Hey," he whispered when his eyes fluttered open seconds after I removed my hand.

"What are you doing here?" I blurted.

Hurt filled his eyes quickly. While he worked on pulling himself to a sitting position with his legs on either side of mine, I wiped my hands down my face. I couldn't bring myself to look back up at him, so I observed my ring like it was the most interesting thing in the world. His large warm hands cradled mine and I felt the tears well up in my eyes.

"What's going on?" he asked quietly.

I shook my head because I knew if I answered him with words I would breakdown. A million different scenes played through my head of how he would react if I told him and none of them were good. Knox started rubbing my hands between his gently, stopping every once in a while to toy with my ring. A few tears escaped and dropped onto our joined hands.

"You know you can tell me anything? I love you and I'm here for you," he reminded me. "We can get through it together."

Those words had more tears spilling. I pulled away from him and stood up. He moved to follow me, I put my finger up and ran upstairs. I went to our room and on the night stand was the ultrasound. I grabbed it and went back down. He hadn't moved other than to put his head in his hands. When he heard me coming closer, he looked up.

I sat back down where I had been with my legs back between his and showed him the picture. Confusion was the first thing to register on his face followed quickly by surprise when I saw his eyes move to the top where my name was. His head came up and I held my breath. A slow smile started to spread across his face and before I knew it that dimple I loved so much was making an appearance.

"We're going to be parents?" he questioned quietly as he grabbed my free hand and intertwined our fingers.

"Yep," I informed him, my voice just as low, nervousness evident as it wavered.

"You were scared to tell me?"

"Every time we had talked about it..." I started, choking up so I had to stop.

"Oh baby," he cooed, quickly pulling me from where I was sitting and onto his lap.

Holding me tightly, he rubbed a hand up and down my

back. I cried, no crying wasn't the right word, I sobbed into his chest. He wasn't mad, that much I knew, and the relief coursed through me. Knox kissed the top of my head and murmured sweet nothings in my ear to calm me and eventually it worked. Leaning over he got me a couple of tissues from the box on the corner of the table in front of us. I mopped up my face, blew my nose, and finally looked up at him again.

"I'm so sorry you felt that way. It's not that I didn't, don't, want children. I already felt like I wasn't giving you the time you deserved. I just worry that I won't be around enough for my kids."

"We have made it work thus far," I said. "However, I completely understand if you want to wait to get married."

"Mackenzie, I put that ring on your finger because I love you and want you in my life forever. Now it just means that much more because you are carrying around a piece of us."

The tears started again. He brought his hand down to my still flat belly and I covered it with my own. Chuckling, he moved to put his mouth close to it to talk to our unborn child.

"Little one we are going to have to work on your mother."

I brought his head up with my hands and kissed him. Putting all the love I had for him into it. The hand that he had had on my belly came up to cup my cheek and he gently ran his thumb back and forth across it when he pulled away.

"Is everything okay?" he asked. "With you and the baby."

"All is well," I let him know as I caressed his face, relishing in the feel of his whiskers beneath my fingers.

"Are you happy?"

"Honestly?" I answered, continuing on when he nodded. "I'm elated."

"Good," he breathed, "because I'm over the moon."

We spent the next few days getting used to the news and talking about things. We agreed that we would wait until I was farther along to tell anyone, but I was nervous I would slip up around the girls. I wasn't good at lying or keeping secrets, despite my ability to surprise Knox on the road. It was nice playing house and having him around. He took care of me, even going so far as to learn how to do chores and doing so without me asking.

"Are you going to be able to keep your mouth shut?" Knox asked with a grin as we drove up my parents' driveway Christmas morning to have brunch with everyone.

"Me? How 'bout you, man with the puffed-out chest?"

He laughed, but didn't deny my statement. Each day that passed found him to be more and more excited about the baby. If we made it another four weeks I would be amazed. Pulling up to the house I noticed that there were some vehicles that I didn't recognize. I glanced at Knox only to find him with the same inquisitive look I had.

Getting out of the car, I leaned into the back and collected the cinnamon roll casserole I had made. Knox instantly relieved me of it when he met me on my side of the car and took my hand in his free one. We made our way up the brick path and were greeted with loud voices as soon as we entered the front door. Walking down the hallway, we both froze when we reached the kitchen.

"Ace? Mom? Dad? Cort?" Knox questioned.

There mingled in with my family and the girls were most of his immediate family and Ace. Sharon rushed over to wrap a stunned Knox in a hug while my mother moved in to take the dish from his hand so he could hug her back. I followed him the rest of the way in the room and Cort came over to pull me into his arms. Bella had been nervous about traveling with the baby so they were spending the holiday with her husband's family. It seemed like forever before all the hugs and kisses were done and food was finally served.

Just as we started to eat, I felt my stomach turn. Clearly the breakfast I had eaten earlier had not sufficed. I rushed to sit down and get food in me, but I wasn't quick enough. I felt the bile start to rise and I bailed out of the room. Knox followed me and held my hair while I lost everything. He wiped my face with a wet cloth and kissed my nose when I was done.

"I think we are going to have to let our secret out," he said tucking a stray piece of hair behind my ear.

"Me too," I admitted. "I may have brought copies of the ultrasound with me."

He shook his head, yet didn't look all that surprised. I cleaned up when I was sure that my stomach wasn't going to revolt again and we rejoined the group. Conversations stopped when we walked into the room and all eyes turned to us. I looked up at Knox who had his arm around my waist and he nodded with a smile, showing his dimple.

"So, we have something to share with you all," I told them, bringing my hands to my belly. "I'm pregnant."

Cheers erupted along with the questions, "How far along are you?" "When are you due?" "When are you getting married?" We answered the questions the best we could and my wonderful man got me a fresh plate of food once I was able to sit down. The buzz picked back up as everyone settled back in and my stomach started to calm once I had inhaled some scrambled eggs and bacon.

A couple of hours later we were spread around the living room watching *A Charlie Brown Christmas*, a tradition in the Shaw household. Eggnog and hot chocolate were served and even though it was a children's movie, we were all mesmerized by what was on the television. I curled into Knox's side and he placed a small kiss on my forehead before turning back to the watch the show. I closed my eyes and inhaled his warmth and smell.

When I opened my eyes, I realized I was the happiest I had ever been in my life. Looking around I took in the people that I loved the most in this world. Meghan sat on the floor in front of me with her head leaning back against the couch; Ace sat on the other side of her leaning back against his hands. Cort was on the other side of Knox; my father sat in his recliner with my mother on his lap. David sat in my mother's recliner with Sharon on his lap; Devon and Alicia were curled up on the other couch, and Matt sat beside them with Kelly sitting on the floor between his legs. I was so blessed to have these people in my life. Putting my hand on my flat belly, I smiled. I couldn't wait to welcome him or her into all of this.

Chapter Nineteen

Present Day

"Things fall into place as they are meant to,
bask in what you are handed and cherish it."

"Ma'am," one of the attendants greeted. "Follow me, please."

The show had wound down after Knox's award. A couple more singers had performed and then everyone had slowly started to stand up and move around. Rebecca had stayed with me awhile, but I had finally shooed her off. I knew she had after-parties to attend. I hadn't been alone long when the man in a suit had materialized at my side. Obviously, my husband had been detained.

I followed the gentleman down the aisle and across the front of the stage. When we got to a door, he opened it and put his hand out to signal me to go ahead. I did and was instantly taken aback. People were everywhere and it was loud. The attendant came back to my side and motioned for me to follow him once again.

We weaved through the crowd and I had to stop numerous times to say hello, receive congratulations, or hug those I knew. It still floored me how quickly some of these people had become like family. The man in the suit patiently waited each time. Finally, we made it to a room off to the side of all the commotion. The door was ajar and I could see Knox inside, along with multiple others. I thanked him and moved forward.

I didn't recognize anyone except my man and Ace. He was being interviewed and held an untouched beer his hand. The smile from earlier hadn't dimmed a bit and his eyes sparkled with excitement. My own smile grew, especially when he spotted me and the dimple I adored so much made an appearance. His free hand waved me in his direction.

Reaching his side, I was instantly wrapped in his arm and tucked against his side. I put one arm around him and the other I placed on his chest. Even though he continued to talk, he looked down and our eyes locked. A chill ran through me and I couldn't wait to celebrate with him alone later. I was so filled with love for this man I almost couldn't contain it.

An hour later we were finally headed out to our car. I stifled a yawn as Knox directed me to our ride with a hand on the small of my back. He gave me an apologetic smile as he gave Ted, our driver, directions to where we were going. I climbed in and put my head back against the seat while I waited. I hoped that we were only going to one place and not ten.

Feeling a tickle on my neck, I slapped it away. It happened again and this time I swung my hand a little harder, only to earn a low chuckle from my husband. I opened my eyes to find him sitting next to me and the car in motion. I rolled my eyes at him, causing him to laugh more.

"So where are we headed to Mr. Entertainer of the Year?" I asked snuggling into his side.

"Just to Cash's," he stated kissing the top of my head. "Then we will head up to the apartment to celebrate alone."

"Sounds perfect," I sighed as his hand slid into the slit of my dress and eased up my thigh.

"Or we could start now," he suggested nibbling up my neck.

"As lovely as that sounds," I giggled, "you need to party with your friends for a while first."

The car came to a stop and Knox moaned in frustration. Straightening my dress, I laughed at him. Even though he was horny as a teenage boy, I knew he was excited to be with everyone. He had worked hard for this and deserved everything that came with it. Knox climbed out when Ted came around and opened the door. Leaning back in slightly, he helped me out and again I was overwhelmed by the crowd and the noise.

People lined the street in front of Knox's bar. It was usually busy, but I had never seen it this way. Obviously everyone had received the memo that this was where some of the elite would be. Two large men in suits guarded the door and let us in with a nod and smile

Inside wasn't quite as bad. There was still a crowd, however you could move freely and not feel like you were going to run into someone at every turn. My husband was immediately swallowed up by a group so I moved to the bar where Red and Jake were busy serving. I found an empty stool and made myself comfortable while I waited.

"The beautiful Mrs. Pride," Red boomed when he spotted me. "The usual?"

"Yes, please, sir," I responded with a grin.

Red was just what you would expect by his name. He was a husky built redhead with a warm smile and sparkling eyes. Knox and his partners had known him growing up and had begged him to come back to work for them. Evidently being a bartender had not been his dream job, yet he was just as much a part of Cash's as the bar itself.

"Here ya go, darlin'," he drawled dropping a beer and a seltzer water in front of me.

I threw him a smile and got up. Drinks in hand, I moved towards Knox. Without interrupting his conversation, I handed him his beer and planted a kiss on his cheek. He gave me a smile that was reserved just for me before shifting his attention back to a man I didn't recognize. I maneuvered my way around and found myself on the dance floor with Rebecca and a few other women I knew.

It was quite a while before the music slowed and I took advantage of it to sneak away and take a breather. I didn't make it very far before I was corralled into a pair of strong arms. The familiar smells of a woodsy cologne and Old Spice deodorant met my nose. Relenting I followed him back to the dance floor and allowed him to pull me into his chest. My arms automatically came up and wrapped around his neck, my fingers instantly going to the hair on the back of his head and threading through it.

I felt his chest rumble under my ear and it took me a minute to realize we were dancing to one of his own songs. "She's All Mine" had become very special to us as a couple in our short time together. Whenever he sang it, it felt like everyone else in the room disappeared and it was just us. I closed my eyes and let him guide me. His hands drew circles on my hips as he continued to sing and I couldn't help but shiver a bit from the friction.

The song ended much too quickly. Before I knew it, we were separating and Knox was being surrounded by people. I quietly slipped around to the side of the dance floor, making my way up the stairs and back to the bar. Red instantly brought me over a water with lemon when I made myself comfortable on a stool. Turning to lean on the bar, I watched what was going on around me.

There was still a fairly large crowd gathered despite the time. Some were gathered in small groups chatting, while others danced away on the floor where I had first met Knox. It was amazing to see so many big names in one place looking so normal, aside from the fancy clothes. They had all welcomed Knox and his hard work warmly in the past year. I was so grateful that they had accepted me as well.

"How are you two doing?" the deep baritone voice I loved so much whispered in my ear.

"We're good," I whispered back looking down at where his hand rested on my growing belly. "Ready for some sleep though."

"Okay my ladies," he said leaning down to plant a kiss on my bump through the dress. "I'm going to let the guys know we are headed upstairs."

I nodded, too tired to argue about him staying later. My feet and lower back ached from the heels, and I suddenly felt like I had been hit by a bus. The craziness of the day was catching up with me and the little girl growing inside me. I rubbed my belly and found Knox watching with a goofy grin on his face while he talked to Cort.

As I looked at him and the amazing business around us, it still surprised me that we were where we were. I had never thought a trip with three of my best friends would have resulted in my meeting a famous country singer, never mind the man I would spend the rest of my life with. His brown eyes met my blue ones as he made his way towards me and I felt that familiar warmth spread through me. Life didn't get much better than this, I marveled, placing my hands back on my belly. I really was living the dream.

* * *

Keep reading for a sneak peek from Knox and Mackenzie's holiday novella *A New Year's Dream...*

A
New Year's
Dream

Marcie Shumway

Chapter 1

Knox

Men are not planners. We fly by the seat of our pants. Women, on the other hand, they plan. They organize. Especially mine, she was the best at that kind of thing. Mackenzie did surprises and I loved that about her.

Now, as I paced my kitchen, I wanted to reciprocate. How the hell was I supposed to do that?! She deserved some time away from the craziness that was our life. We deserved alone time as a couple. Again, how was I supposed to do this? Wait. I had people. Being a famous country singer meant I had people.

"Come on," I muttered seconds later, the other end of my cell phone ringing in my ear. "Answer."

"Do you know what time it is?" The voice on the other end growled.

I grimaced and glanced at the glowing numbers on the microwave, 2:00 AM shone blue in the dark room. Oops. Having a three-year-old that didn't like to sleep and being on tour really messed with one's sleep cycles.

"Ace, man," I stammered. "I'm so sorry."

"Ellie still isn't sleeping, huh?" came the chuckled reply.

"When she wants to," I sighed. "Kenz says it is worse when I'm home. She's afraid she is going to miss something."

"Well, if that doesn't break your heart."

"Don't I know it."

"So, what's up otherwise?"

"Never mind," I mumbled apologetically. "I'll call you later, at a more reasonable hour."

"Knox," Ace chided. "I'm awake."

"Fine."

"What do you need?"

"I want to surprise Mackenzie and take her away for a long weekend for New Year's."

"I'm not going to ask why you waited until now to plan this."

"Don't. I've got child and animal care covered," I told him. "I just need a place for us to stay."

"Cabin or room?"

"Cabin."

"Maine?"

"Yep."

"Got it. Now let me sleep."

The line went dead in my ear, and I laughed.

Ace was my best friend, my right-hand man, and the person I was the closest to other than my brother. He'd been my manager my entire career and could move mountains. Well, I liked to think so anyway.

Running my hand through my hair, I made my way back upstairs. My daughter's door stood ajar, so I poked my head in. She was in the same place I'd left her, sleeping soundly with her white noise machine running. It seemed to be the only thing that kept her asleep these days. A soft smile came to my lips as I took her in. She was perfect.

Ellie Rose Pride entered the world two weeks early, screaming like a banshee. Ten fingers, ten toes, and looks that resembled both of us. Her hair was her mothers, her eyes mine, and slowly I could see other features of ours coming out. That little girl had me wrapped around her finger and she knew it. A little sigh in her sleep broke me from my reverie.

I shifted and walked to our bedroom. My wife had turned over. She faced the wall with her back to the door. I grinned. Pulling my t-shirt over my head, I moved to the side of the bed. I slid under the covers and spooned her.

Naturally, Kenz leaned back into me. Her ass wiggled against me. My cock instantly twitched in my boxers in response. I slipped one leg between hers and felt her heat, she was ready for me. Nibbling on Kenz's bare shoulder, I ran a hand over her hip, tracing down to the front of her panties. The woman was soaked.

One thing about our relationship, the physical spark never faltered. My body reacted to her now the same way it had when we first met. That piece we never worked on; it came naturally. It also made the baby making process that much easier.

While Ellie had been a surprise, we quickly decided we wanted our children close in age. Mackenzie knew I couldn't take too much time off the road, but she was willing to take me when she could get me. Our support system at home amazing and I'd updated my bus to one family size.

Mackenzie's hand reached back for me. Before she hurt herself, I released my shaft from my boxers. Her fingers were warm against my skin, and I pulsed in her hand. Slapping her away playfully, I pulled down her underwear and slid home.

Our movements weren't rushed, a steady rhythm set. Hands and fingers rubbed and gripped. My lips traveled her skin, while she bit hers to keep her moans in check. When I reached around to massage her generous breasts, I felt her interior muscles clasp around me. She was so close. I knew what she needed.

My hand moved south and found her clit. Swollen and sensitive, I flicked it gently. She spasmed, setting off the tingle in my spine. Nipping and sucking on the spot just under her ear, I started insistently working her nub. When she clamped around me like a vice, I went over with her.

"You okay, baby?" I asked after we laid there for a bit, still joined.

"Oh yeah," she breathed with a light laugh.

I smiled and placed a kiss on her neck. She giggled and pulled her shoulder up. Then I heard her yawn. She slapped a hand over her mouth to block the noise causing me to chuckle. Sliding from her, I went to the bathroom to clean up and wet a cloth with warm water for her.

Mackenzie sighed softly when I returned and ran the cloth over her. Those little noises went straight to my heart. Once she was clean, I tossed the washcloth toward the bathroom and climbed back into bed. Within seconds of curling myself back around her, my body finally relaxed, giving in to the lack of sleep.

* * *

Doo Doo Doo

Groaning, I rolled over, away from the noise.

Doo Doo Doo

No, I was not answering that. I reached out for my wife and found the bed empty. A giggle came from downstairs, traveling up and through the partially open door. She was in the kitchen with Ellie.

Doo Doo Doo

I finally reached over to the nightstand and grabbed my phone. Ace's name came across the screen. I cursed at him under my breath.

"You'd better be dying," I muttered.

"Kettle black?" He chuckled.

I rubbed a hand down my face and opened my eyes to stare at the ceiling. He was right. I did it to him just hours ago.

"What's up?"

"That's better." I could hear the smile in his voice. "I found you a place. It is two hours north in Jacobstown. Cabin AirBNB."

"That's perfect," I replied.

"I booked Friday to Monday," he continued. "They aren't booked again until the end of the following week, so if you want a couple extra days you can have them."

"I'll check with her parents."

"I'm emailing your itinerary as we speak to your email address with the subject line TOUR."

"That'll work."

"Anything else, brother?"

"All good, man."

"Later."

I hung up and grinned like a fool. I couldn't wait to surprise Mackenzie. After the past few years, it was time for us to be alone and for me to return the favor.

Chapter 2

Mackenzie

Case shifted under me and pawed at the ground. I patted his black neck, apologizing for my distant mind. Tapping my heels against his sides lightly, he moved forward eagerly. I shook my head to clear it. Time to concentrate on the task at hand.

When Knox officially made Maine his home base, there'd been two things he wanted to add to the property. The studio wasn't a surprise. The man wanted to be able to do anything he did in Nashville at home. An indoor riding arena had been a surprise, a welcome one. He knew how much riding calmed my frayed nerves when it came to my writing.

Today was no exception. It was release day. The anticipated ending to my beloved second series. It was a book that would tear at the heartstrings with an ending no one, not even me, would have anticipated. Meghan, my PA and best friend, was in our office at the controls. After I started pacing, she banished me. Knox and Ellie were off spending the day together, so I'd turned to my first love. My horses.

Since I hadn't ridden in weeks, Case, my quarter horse

cross was testing me. I didn't blame him, but quickly reminded him of his manners. Each time, he responded with a snort and a toss of his head. His antics made me laugh slightly. He'd been a rescue and the owners he was taken from couldn't provide any history. He turned out to be a diamond in the rough.

"Nice try," I admonished the gelding with another squeeze.

Case wanted to do as little work as possible, which was his usual. The boy liked to eat and hang out with his buddies. Exercise was a chore. That was exactly why I'd picked him, he made me work for it.

We walked a warmup pattern and moved into a posting trot when he was ready. I maneuvered him over some poles I'd laid out and in large circles around barrels in the corners. Keeping his mind guessing what came next seemed to be the only way he liked to do ring work. Trails were more his forte, but this time of the year they were too icy and covered in snow.

"Little more speed, bud," I mumbled, more to myself than him.

Another nudge with a kissing noise and he grunted his way into a canter. I smirked. It was slow and easy. Moving with him, I used my seat to keep him going. We cut across the ring and reversed direction, the gelding changing leads without me even asking. I scratched his neck lightly with a couple fingers.

The door to the arena opened and shut quietly behind us. Case's ears flickered at the noise, but he continued on. As we neared where we started, I sat deeper in the saddle, and he instantly dropped his pace. I scratched him harder this time, praising him.

"He looks so good," my mom commented when we got closer.

"Better every winter it seems."

She nodded in agreement. Case beelined it for his grandma

and tucked his head against her chest for sympathy. Anything to get him out of work. I shook my head with a laugh.

"Can I have a turn?" She asked, running her hands down his cheeks.

"Be my guest."

I hopped down and pulled my helmet off to hand to her. She took it, along with Case's reins, and headed for the mounting block. Putting my gloves back on since I wasn't moving my hands, I plopped myself down into one of the chairs along the outside rail of the building.

She got on, causing Case to sigh heavily and my mother to laugh. The sight made me smile. The love for horses came from her. She had them growing up and when I asked for lessons as a child, she happily obliged.

"You hiding from release day?" She questioned as she set the horse moving in the opposite direction that I had been.

"Eh." I shrugged. "Meghan kicked me out."

Another laugh.

"I'm glad I'm not the only one you drive crazy when your book goes live."

I rolled my eyes, but gave her a good-natured smile. I knew I wasn't an overly fun person to be around when my books went out to the masses. Writing was my passion. Once I got flowing with a story it was hard to get me out of it. Editing, I tolerated as it was part of the process of perfecting my gift to my readers. Releasing, I despised it. I would grow anxious and continuously jump around the social media platforms looking for what people were saying and read reviews, a number one no-no for authors.

Snuggling deeper into my jacket, I watched my mother work Case. While I loved to ride, I also enjoyed seeing other people on my horses. Each one had their own personality and seemed to adjust themselves to whoever their riders were. Case was a pleaser for everyone, he just got bored quickly in the arena. He had been a rescue with no background, but sometimes I wondered if they tried to make him a show horse and he failed. Max, my high school graduation present, was a chestnut quarter horse that had been there, done that. Anyone could get on him, whether they knew how to ride or not, and he would take care of them. The last one, Gem, I'd gotten when a family in town was going through a divorce. He was a little bit more of a hot ticket as a thoroughbred, but he was fun. Not afraid of much and always ready to move regardless of where.

I checked my watch as she started to cool him down. It was closing in on five o'clock. Chore time. I'd been hiding outside since lunch and it was probably time to head back inside soon anyway. My mother finished up, hopped off the horse, and the three of us made our way to the barn. Grateful Knox connected the arena to my barn since it was chilly. I could see the other two in the windows watching us. Shaking my head with a laugh, I directed my mom to the cross ties that had Case's halter and brushes. She started to take care of him as I finished prepping the stalls for them for the night.

A radio played a country station for background music at all times and I hummed along with it. My mother joined in. My heart swelled. No matter what Meghan gave me for news about release day when I got back into the house, this time right here made the day worth it. I had family, friends, and a wonderful husband that supported me in all that I did.

We finished at the same time and once I checked Case to find him cool, he was put in his stall to start his supper. I rolled the overhead door up and the other two popped their heads over the gate to greet me. Cooing to them, I reminded them they needed to back up before I could open it to let them in. Pushing each other, they moved over. I unhooked and swung the metal gate just enough for them to fit in individually. I got that "hurry up" look from Gem, who waited patiently for me to tell them they could come forward. When I did, the two walked in and went right into their stalls on their best behavior.

It took time and repetition, but I'd instilled a few things like that into them over the years. As an author, I sometimes traveled for signings, so others had to help care for them. During the warmer months, they lived outside and had a run-in making it much easier. In the winter, like now, with snow on the ground and temps below 40 most of the time, they came into the barn at night and needed to be blanketed on bitter cold days.

"Ready to go face the music?" My mom asked as she came up beside me at Gem's stall.

Letting out a deep sigh, I nodded. She put her arm around my shoulder and gave it a squeeze.

"You've got this," she whispered in my ear before kissing my temple.

We double checked the boys' stall locks and headed out. Lights glowed from the house and my heart flipped. The sight never got old. When we approached the sliding glass door into the kitchen, I stopped short and my mother ran into me with an *oofff*. Meghan was dancing around the kitchen with Ellie on her hip and Knox was taking takeout from bags on the counter. While it shouldn't have surprised me since this had become a release day ritual, there was an underlying excitement that could be felt through the glass.

I grabbed the door and slid it open quickly. They both stopped and looked at me, Ellie instantly putting her arms out for me to take her. I looked back and forth between my husband and my best friend. Suddenly, the whole room went wild, the two of them were talking at once and Ellie started screeching. My mother quickly took her from Meghan, and I gripped my friend by the forearms to get her to stop moving.

"Slow down," I told her. "I can't understand you."

"You.Are.A.Bestseller." She annunciated each word.

Knox wrapped his arms around me from behind as I stood looking at her, my mouth gaping open. Shock. That was the only thing I could register. I felt my knees go weak and Knox's chest rattled against my back as he chuckled. I'd done it. After 25 books, all self-published, I'd made the list every author longed to. I didn't care what number, I was on it.

"Oh my god!" I finally managed to get out and pulled her to me.

Knox released me so we could dance around together. My mother was next to us, cheering with Ellie. The next thing I knew, my kitchen was full of my family. My brother, my father, my friends Kelly and Alicia had all shown up. I assumed that Meghan called them. Tears wet my cheeks and I hugged everyone.

"Okay, do you want to know where you were at last I checked?"

I shook my head. I didn't want to ruin this. I wanted to feel like this forever.

"Tough." She laughed. "You were at number 5!"

More cheers. More hugs. More tears.

Everything passed in a blur. We finally settled down and started dishing food onto plates. My brother put Ellie in her highchair while everyone sat down to start eating. I realized I'd forgotten a water and snuck away from the table to the refrigerator. As I turned around with a bottle of water in hand, I nearly jumped out of my skin to find my husband directly behind me. He pinned me between him and the metal doors.

"So, since I have a feeling you are going to be distracted most of the night, I wanted to share my surprise with you."

"Another one," I all but purred. The excitement, coupled with his intoxicating scent, had my lady parts stirring.

He chuckled and tapped me on the nose with his pointer finger. "Not that naughty girl."

"Spoil sport," I teased.

"There will be plenty of time for that," he said with a wicked grin. "I'm taking you away for New Year's. Three days and two nights, just us, in a cabin."

"Like US, US?!" I asked.

"Just you and me, baby," he whispered, leaning in and brushing his lips against mine. "No Ellie, no family, and no friends."

My night had capped out. I didn't think things could get any better. I'd been wanting time alone with Knox for as long as I could remember. With us trying for a second baby, it had been hard working around Ellie's weird sleep schedule. Plus, it would be wonderful to just reconnect with him.

"I can't wait," I whispered back and returned the kiss. "Hope you are ready for me."

"Ditto."

* * *

A New Year's Dream is available on Amazon - in ebook and paperback!

About the Author

Marcie Shumway is a small-town girl, born and raised in Maine. She resides on a family owned farm just miles from where she grew up. Her four furbabies are her first loves, but they are followed closely by her writing, apple pie, and chocolate.

Marcie started writing short stories in middle school for her classmates to enjoy. They were always love stories with happy endings and spurred her dream of being a published author. Chasing that dream as an adult, she continues to write stories for her readers to love. An avid reader herself, Marcie thrives on the books of her favorite authors and when not writing, can be found curled up in her favorite spot with a good book in hand.

Also by Marcie Shumway

The Finding Series

Finding the Way Home

Finding the Way to Your Heart

Finding the Way Back

Living the Dream

The Comeback Series

The Return

The Unknown

The Wait

The Secret

425 Madison Series

His Last Ride

Her Last Love

Remembering the Spirit of Christmas